Suitors

FOR THE
PROPER MISS

JEN GEIGLE JOHNSON

LORDS FOR THE SISTERS OF SUSSEX SERIES

The Duke's Second Chance
The Earl's Winning Wager
Her Lady's Whims and Whimsies
Suitors for the Proper Miss
Pining for Lord Lockhart
The Foibles and Follies of Miss Grace

Follow Jen's Newsletter for a free book and to stay up to date on her releases. https://www.subscribepage.com/y8p6z9

FOLLOW JEN

Charmed by His Lordship
The antics of a fake friendship

Tabitha's Folly
Four over-protective brothers

To read Damen's Secret
The Villain's Romance

Follow her Newsletter

1

The path between the castle where Miss Lucy Standish lived and the stables was long and windy and well-travelled by herself. Trees overhung in a perfect canopy. They blocked out all but the heaviest raindrops she'd discovered when caught once in a downpour.

Today, the sky was a beautiful blue. And the very air drew her to the stables and her horse. And, if she were being honest, to Mr. Sullivan. The son of their stablemaster offered the perfect balance against all the other pressures she felt. He was easy, hardworking, and focused on the horses. When she wanted to go think of nothing else, she would listen to him talk. The Irish accent was more prominent in his father, but the tiny song in his voice often calmed her like the rise and fall of a ship on low waves. They weren't friends, precisely, but he was good to humor her presence while he worked.

Miss Lucy Standish adjusted her gloves so that no wrinkles marred their appearance. She wasn't like her sister Kate, conscious of fashion and appearances because she particularly *liked* accessories. Nor was she concerned with staying on top of the latest so she could write a column about the most recent color or cut of a man's jacket.

Though Lucy loved her sister fiercely, she and Kate were different indeed.

But Lucy *did* care that her clothing was precisely and perfectly appropriate. And she knew that in this particular riding habit, bonnet, gloves, and dainty boots, she painted a perfect—and fetching—picture.

And why should she care how she dressed when at home? Here on her estate with no one about but the staff in the stables?

Because the words of the Duchess of Sussex rang in her ears more often than not. For some reason this morning, they were clanging especially loudly. Lucy could see in her mind's eye the duchess's long finger pointed across the room. "That Lucy. She is the one of you who can catch herself a duke, mark my words. I was once just like your dear Lucy."

Lucy had studied her, many times in point of fact, and had found nothing in the woman remotely similar to herself. But who was she to argue the point when a royal duchess had taken a liking to her?

And marrying a duke was all that Lucy wanted.

A huff of dissatisfied breath rose up as a tiny cloud into the air. The weather was chillier than she would have expected for March. Her face felt tight from the cold. A ride, long and chilling, would awaken her to a sense of duty. Not just any duke would do. Noble blood in the Sussex line would at last purge them of the stain of their poverty. Lucy's sister June had married Morley, an earl. Lucy often tasted the sound of those words, judging them against her previously deter-mined goals. And she found them wanting.

An earl was a blessing for them all, to be sure. But a

duke would solidify their security. Gerald, their friend and the Duke of Granbury, and his wife Amelia were like family, had treated them as such, and were some of the dearest people of her acquaintance, but his dukedom did not reach them in lineage and none of their children or grandchildren were likely to benefit except possibly through marriage one day. She was remarkably ahead of herself in her plans, but Lucy was, in fact, a remarkable planner. And she knew of all the sisters, it was up to her to marry a man of eminence.

Lord Fellon's face came into her mind. He was handsome. Everyone agreed. And he would be the Duke of Stratton, nephew to Lord Hallings who was the son of a royal duke.

And he had shown an interest in Lucy. When Gerald had extended his assistance to include dowries for the sisters, Lord Fellon's interest had grown. And she couldn't blame him for that. When she considered what that man offered in a marriage as far as connections and title, a dowry was the least she could do. That and offer up herself as a woman of impeccable taste, deportment, and ability to be a duchess.

These thoughts exhausted her this morning.

A familiar tuneful whistle, coming from the barn, picked up her pace. And her cheeks lifted from the force of her sudden grin.

The door flung open, and the source of her distraction led Maple, a beautiful chestnut mare, out of the barn. Mr. Conor Sullivan. He had not seen her as yet. And so she took a moment to unabashedly stare. He seemed taller every time she saw him. His curls were damp, his face contented, and his lips puckered in a lively whistle. She recognized the tune. Could he sing? No doubt. They didn't often speak of anything besides horses, so even though she'd been coming out to the stables every day when home, she really didn't know much about the man.

He led Maple to a post, tied her there, and turned presumably to get another. Good humor sparkled in his eyes.

For the hundredth time, Lucy wondered what it would be like to live so carefree a life. Conor Sullivan never seemed troubled. She found herself looking for excuses to be in his presence, hoping some of his ease would wear off on her.

His eyes caught hers and he stood taller, some of his ease shifting behind the servant's mask they all wore. Then he dipped his head. "Good morning, Miss Lucy."

"Good morning to you, Mr. Sullivan."

"Can I get Firestone ready for you this morning?"

"This morning, I think I'd like to ride Devil's Nape."

His expression closed off even further. She shouldn't have done it. She shouldn't tease, but something about this man's perfect ease, his insistence at remaining perfectly proper, dared her to agitate him.

"He's not yet fed this morning. Or watered. I should be getting to him shortly, maybe in another hour..." Did she catch a hint of challenge in his expression?

A part of her wanted to laugh, but instead, she shook her head. "Surely he can be next in your preparations? Eat some oats while we saddle him up?"

And there was another point in her favor. She could saddle her own horses, which he well knew since he was the one who had taught her, at her insistence. She preferred to do the job herself and would have all the time, except that it simply wasn't proper. And in all things, Lucy was proper.

Almost all things. She eyed Mr. Sullivan, wondering what he would do next. They both knew that Lord Morley had forbidden Devil's Nape be ridden by any of the sisters, by anyone but himself except perhaps for Mr. Sullivan, until he was a more reliable mount.

But Lucy was itching to take him out. And at the moment, she wanted nothing more than a reckless and fiery storm across the meadow.

"That we could. He'd appreciate the oats, to be sure." He studied her a moment, a rare connection where their eyes met. His were usually down, in a respectful servant's gaze. "Do we expect his lordship this morning?"

"Not for hours yet." She stood taller.

Watching the movement in Mr. Sullivan's jaw, just a twitch at the back, made her grin and desist in her torment. "But I suspect I could be just as pleased riding my mare. Could I get Firestone?"

He dipped his head. "Certainly, miss."

As he turned from her, she called him back. "Might I ride with you for company as you exercise the others?" She wasn't supposed to go out alone. And she much preferred Mr. Sullivan to any of the footmen. His wealth of knowledge about horses alone made him far more interesting than most.

His hesitation was barely perceptible, but it was there. And she wanted to erase it tenfold.

"Lord Morley has encouraged us to ride accompanied. And since you are already preparing to go out?" She widened her eyes in a hopeful kind of pleading gesture. She shouldn't have. But something about his matter-of-fact reactions to things, his ease and comfort were just what she needed this morning, that and a person so completely unrelated to the ton and the coming season and the climb to find a man of title; she found the thought refreshing. Perhaps she'd even ask him what he thought of her latest suspicion, that the moon and stars followed patterns of placement in the sky, something she could never bring up in a ballroom.

He turned back. "Certainly. All the horses could use a ride."

She inwardly thrilled but outwardly simply nodded her head.

Firestone pranced when she saw Lucy.

"Oh, how's my pretty lady? Hm?" She reached a hand out and stroked her mare's nose. "You ready for a run?" She leaned closer to whisper. "We need to show Mr. Sullivan what we've got this morning. No holding back."

Firestone's responding nicker made her smile. "That's a girl. That's my pretty lady."

"What are you two planning over there?" Mr. Sullivan's surprisingly playful tone caught her attention immediately, and when she glanced up, she saw the source.

He led out Devil's Nape himself.

Her eyebrows rose up to her hairline, but she didn't ask. When he went about tightening the straps as though he were to ride the stallion, she put hands on hips. "What is this?"

"Lord Morley has asked that I ride him." The complete challenge in his face, the manner in which he went about getting Devil's Nape ready as though nothing were amiss brought her head back in a laugh, open and free from restraint.

Though the air still felt cold, she was warmed to her toes. "Did he now?"

Mr. Sullivan nodded. "He did." Then their stable hand surprised her and stepped closer, leaning his head near, and whispered, "And if we happened to swap mounts partway through the ride, who's to know?" His eyes, full of adventure, captured her immediately. And then he winked.

And she wasn't certain she'd be able to breathe again for many minutes.

But he went back to whistling as if nothing were amiss in her air-depleted world.

Soon they were both on their horses, she having used a mounting block and he just swinging up as if he were born to ride.

And, she reminded herself, he *had* been born to ride. He was a stable hand. His father their stablemaster. The family had been working in Brighton for generations. Or so she'd heard.

And she had no business being so interested in the man anyway.

If only he wasn't so easy to be with, so…comforting in an unsettling way.

Firestone shifted underneath her.

Devil's Nape lifted his front legs off the ground in a small dance.

"I think we need to get moving." She laughed. Then she patted Firestone. "You ready, girl?"

Firestone leapt forward, and Lucy shouted in surprise, but she couldn't be more pleased. "We're off!"

Mr. Sullivan with Devil's Nape were immediately at her side. He was keeping the stallion in check to ride at her pace.

She clucked. None of that. With a nudge from her foot, Firestone leapt to a full-on run, and Lucy let her bonnet slip from her head, tied at her neck and flapping on her back. Her pins were likely fighting for their position in her hair, and she would soon have her hairstyle completely ruined. But she didn't care. She let go of the reins, and with hands out to her sides and teeth chilled from smiling, she rode in a desperate act of pure freedom. For who was there to see? She could be and do and say anything she wanted right now. And she refused to ask herself if future duchesses behaved in such an uncouth manner.

Mr. Sullivan immediately caught up to her again at her side, confound him.

With one look at the competitive challenge on his face, she determined that every ounce of today's happiness would be bought by a win in a race against Mr. Sullivan. She leaned forward. And Firestone responded.

She loved her mare.

With every reaching lunge of her horse's legs, Lucy urged her for one more. They tore across the fields and pastures, leaping over fences, across the immense stretch of land that led all the way to the cliffside at the sea.

And she gloried in it.

For a moment, she thought she'd lost Mr. Sullivan, but he appeared out of the corner of her eye to both her consternation and her exhilaration.

"Oh no, you don't." Her sudden burst of speed earned a laugh from him.

Many minutes later, still neck and neck, they approached the cliffs, and he eased back on Devil's Nape, which made her do the same, satisfied that he had slowed first. Now at a walk, he rode beside her, close. Close enough she could hear his breathing.

She too must be out of breath.

Nothing was said for many minutes while the horses ambled along and the sea stretched out at her side. The wind had picked up. Lucy supposed her hair was doing its best representation of a hoyden. And she was warmed through. What a glorious morning.

At last, she nodded to him. "Devil's Nape is an excellent animal."

"I agree. But Firestone was not making it easy for him." Lucy smiled and patted her horse. "We are alike in that." He studied her, and she saw quite a few questions cross his face, but he held his tongue, as was his typical response. Tosh. Today, she did not want to let him hide away in silence. She was of a mood to pull him out of himself, to cause a little trouble in his perfectly staid and in-control manners.

"And are you like your mount? Like the noble and rascally Devil's Nape?" She laughed when she said it but inwardly gasped at her bold behavior. She waved her hand. "I apologize. I'm..." What was she? "I'm..." She turned to him. "I'm just in need of a good laugh." With a shrug, she turned away.

"I'm nothing like this animal." His voice surprised her. She had no expectation he would respond at all. "He's asking to be sold at auction for his stubborn antics."

"Oh no? Then are you more like Firestone here?"

"No, I think she is perfectly suited to you. I'm..." His face turned contemplative, and in it, she recognized intelligence and ambition, two things she'd never considered in her stable hand before. "I'm afraid I'm not like any of our horses." He grinned. "I consider myself more their master." With that, he shrugged and laughed to himself.

"Ho ho! Well, then you are in the perfect occupation."

"Probably so."

They both slowed and turned to face the water. She slid from her horse. "Shall we? I'm of a mind to walk the cliffs. If you like, you can take my horse back and alert someone to come in a carriage?" She secretly hoped he would stay, but she was aware of his actual occupation, or she assumed at least that he had tasks to complete.

"I am happy to stay. I don't think Lord Morley would take too kindly to me leaving you here without a horse on the cliffs."

She looked away to hide her blush. "Too true. Then I apologize for keeping you."

He took the reins of both horses. "I'm happy to be of service." His face was completely blank when he said those words, and she wondered if he truly was happy to be of service. Did the servants enjoy their jobs? She chided herself for the direction of her thoughts. The happiness and inner workings of the minds of her servants was not somewhere she should be spending her suppositions. She would be far better suited divining manners in which to win the heart of Lord Fellon.

She sighed. She had spent countless minutes wondering about him, and frankly, she was exhausted at the thought of what on earth could win the heart of a duke.

The irony that it pushed her curiosity toward their stable hand was not lost on her, but she'd always thought Mr. Sullivan of interest. Their family actually talked of him and his father often as being a good, respectable family.

"Good people. Salt of the earth," Morley would often say.

They walked toward the very edge of the green. She looked out over the water, her hair now blowing in its full length behind her. She gave it no mind except to recognize she enjoyed the sensation.

When she turned to Mr. Sullivan, he was not looking out at the sea but straight at her. And he didn't look away when she noticed.

"Thank you." She smiled. "I find I very much needed this."

"This...what?" If I may be so bold...what about this did you need?" His question came from earnest eyes, a gaze that studied her as she thought of her response.

What exactly about this afternoon had she most needed? "I think it was any number of things. Being out on Firestone, naturally."

"Of course." He waited.

"And the freedom to just let my hair go, bonnet flailing in the breeze." She laughed.

And he looked even more curious but, as usual, did not pursue the subject.

"Please, ask what you would like to."

"What do you mean?"

"I see these almost words on your lips." When she said the word "lips," she sucked in a breath, recognizing anew the intimacy of their conversation. But she tried to brush it off as if it were nothing. "I see you wanting to say more, and you do not," she challenged him, waiting.

He seemed to consider her for a moment, opened his mouth, and then closed it again.

"See!" She laughed.

And to her delight, his cheeks turned the tiniest bit of pink before he joined her in laughter and looked away. "Miss Standish. Perhaps you have forgotten for a moment the difference in our stations, but I cannot." He dipped his head. "Forgive me, if I must never forget."

She held her breath a moment and then nodded in resignation. "As you should. Thank you."

"You are most welcome." He studied her again, his eyes suddenly full of humor. "But if I *were* to forget, if I were to speak out of turn for but a moment, I would ask, however boldly I might sound, if a woman enjoys riding with her hair down so much, why does she simply not do so as often as she likes?"

"And if you were so bold as to ask such a question, would it be better I did not answer, to keep us both from the impropriety of this direction in our conversation?"

"That would be entirely up to you. You could perhaps suppose what you might answer were you to deviate from your carefully proper persona."

She gasped. "And why do you think it merely a persona? Am I not carefully proper?"

His gaze travelled over the length of her, from her likely very wild hair to the tips of her toes and then nodded. "As you say." He dipped his head in the perfect subservient bow. One which needled her to no end in this moment.

She huffed inwardly before choosing her words. "If I were to deign to respond to such an outlandish question, I would say that I am most certainly concerned with the manner in which I present myself. I am constantly aware of the lowness of our poverty and station but a few months past, a year now, and I see it as my duty to raise the family back into the ranks of the nobility." She looked at him, knowing what she must say next, the phrase oft repeated in her mind over and over. "A duchess would never behave so."

Instead of laughing or teasing or asking anything further, his eyes filled with compassion and a tinge of sorrow. "Very well. Understood." He cleared his throat, looking out at the ocean. "Then I am pleased to have been witness and companion to this most reckless of all afternoons, and I swear I will carry the secret of it to my grave."

His mouth twitched, at the corner, just the tiniest amount,

and by that, she knew he was making fun. But he understood. She knew he grasped everything she was trying to say perfectly, and something about their shared moment filled her with gratitude. She spread her arms out to the ocean. "Do you ever wish to sail out to sea and never return?"

The hand on her arm surprised her and sent a strong, happy shiver all the way to her center. Her eyes widened as he tugged at her.

"Pardon me, miss, but please, you are standing so close to the edge."

Her toes were indeed curling over the edge of the rock jutting out into open space down to the rocks below.

Her very core ached with a new kind of concern, and she stepped away with a hand on her heart. "Thank you. I didn't notice."

He nodded. "I feel much better now." Then he smiled, most of his formality returning. But a flush to his cheek told her he had been well and truly concerned. "In answer to your question, no, I do not wish to sail away. I think I belong to the land. And the animals who roam upon it. The brief moments I've ever spent fishing with my uncle are moments that I enjoy but long to return from sooner rather than later."

"Interesting." She wondered if it was the ocean that appealed so much or merely the idea of escaping. Whichever it was, hopping on a boat and never looking back did seem rather like a good idea at the moment, and she had no idea why.

With an unsettled sigh, she turned back to face the land. "Perhaps we should be getting back."

"Yes, miss." He turned the horses around so that the saddle was more accessible to her. "Would you like some help up?"

And her extraordinarily errant heart skipped a few of its regular beats before she could find a steady voice to reply. "Yes, please."

His hands cupped her hips, one on each side, and their strength astounded her. With a quick lift, she was up on the saddle and adjusting her skirts.

He had looked away, thankfully, so as to miss her warm face and clearly flustered reaction to him. He was up on his saddle in another moment, and they were making their way back across the grass.

A part of her knew that she could race him, knew that she might even enjoy it, knew she might beat him.

But she didn't.

The other part knew that their ride would end all the sooner, and she most desperately did not wish for that.

For then, she'd be tying her hair back in a low-lying, appropriate knot. She'd be saying and doing things a duchess might, and she'd be constantly in check, morning to night, while she practiced to be exactly appropriate and just a bit proud.

And right now, everything about her dreams to one day be a duchess felt more confining than anything else.

2

L ucy entered the house with her messy wild hair that was still full of knots tied behind her in a bun. She would have to head straight up the stairs to get that situated directly.

But Grace came around the corner. "Lucy!" She always seemed to dance her words; her whole body would swing in anticipation or something. And usually, it was such a mood lifter, and Lucy appreciated her youngest sister's exuberance. But today, she kind of wanted to run and hide her appearance until she got it all sorted out.

"Come." Grace linked her hands onto Lucy's elbow. "Let's go join the others."

"Why? What's going on?"

"We just haven't had the whole of us together in many months." She pouted. "I miss Kate, and she's finally here. Logan is off with Morley and Gerald. It's just us women at home right now."

Lucy's outlook brightened. Even though her appearance was still bothering her, she ignored any remaining pings of concern. She almost skipped alongside Grace's happy steps. "Where is everyone?"

"June's room."

Of course. Lucy smiled. And they picked up their pace.

Grace giggled, and then when they were halfway up the stairs, she called, "I found her! Lucy is here too!"

"Get that girl in here!" Charity called. Lucy's most bossy sister. She was just so…different from most other women Lucy knew. And she loved her for it. And kind of feared for her, and marveled at her courage. Just as Lucy tried to follow every single one of society's expectations carefully, Charity seemed to fight against each one with a vengeance.

"I'm coming!" Lucy called.

She and Grace ran into the room and leapt up onto the bed like they had as young girls.

All the sisters inched closer.

Their eldest, June, hugged a pillow to her chest. "Oh, sisters! I'm so happy we are all here." She looked at each one, and Lucy felt her throat go tight. "Me too. This is nice." She nudged Kate. "How are you and Logan?"

"Oh, we're wonderful!" She pointed to June. "She told me marriage would be wonderful, and she is so right. He's even better now that we're married."

Charity looked like she was going to tease them all about their fascination with men but surprisingly seemed instead to be listening more intently.

Interesting.

June's form had enlarged quite a bit. The baby wasn't coming yet, but he or she seemed to want to make their presence known. And June's tall form had hidden it well at first, but now, her stomach was larger than they had ever imagined a stomach could be. Lucy was more than excited for the new little one to enter their home.

She looked from sister to sister and couldn't help but feel her heart expand even more. June had married the best of men, Morley, and the two of them, with his best friend, the Duke of Granbury, had saved them all, gifting them this amazing, beautiful castle to live in. Renovations were still underway to bring it to its past glory.

Once a castle owned by William the Conqueror himself, they were discovering more about themselves and him and their family line every day.

Charity, the second eldest, spent her days studying and planning and joining with others in radical ideas and thoughts. If bluestocking hadn't been invented before Charity, they might have named the term for her. She was always found at every social situation surrounded by men. Perhaps others might be envious, looking on, but Lucy and her sisters knew that she was engaging them in interesting conversation and challenging their beliefs on nearly every subject. It seemed to work well for her as she had no end of offers to dance and visitors during calling hours, but Lucy admitted to secretly wondering if any of these men were actually considering her as a potential marriage prospect or merely preferred her conversation. Her stunning red curls and pert nose on a heart-shaped face certainly aided in her acceptance.

Grace was the youngest of their group and not quite out in society. They'd allowed her to join them for close-knit groups, for activities and things, or one very well-chaperoned ball, but she wanted more and more to be involved in the social events they all participated in. The day would come when she would have her own season.

Lucy sighed. She hadn't really had an official season. And

she was beginning to think that might be what was needed for her to secure a husband.

Kate still wrote her Whims and Fancies column. Lucy was proud of her. She used her fascination with fashion to help other women know what was truly beautiful. Many read her column before going to the modiste to order their next ball gown. Logan, her husband, was just as aware and educated about the finer points of fashion. The two were so deeply in love and happy that Lucy sometimes longed for what they had instead of what she sought.

And why could she not have a love match with a duke's son as well as any other?

Time would tell.

June said something she didn't quite hear, and everyone turned to her.

"What was that?" Lucy smiled.

"She said, what were you doing this morning gone so long?"

"Oh." She laughed and surprised herself with the warmth of her cheeks making themselves known. *Goodness.* "I went for a ride. It was lovely. I was on my way to fix the damage to my hair and change out of this habit, but Grace said I'd been summoned."

"And we're so happy you came straight away." Kate rested a hand on her arm.

"I am as well. It's not like we have visitors who will see me in such a state."

Charity huffed. "As if that even matters. If a person holds that high of an opinion on your appearance to allow it to change their very opinion of you, then who would want such a person in their life?"

Kate looked as though she might have an opinion about Charity's strong words, but she kept her tongue.

June laughed. "And have we decided on the name of my new babe?"

"Francis if she's a girl. And Theodore if he's a boy." Grace grinned.

"No, they must be named after some of the greats in our books. Macbeth. Joan. You can leave off 'of Arc' if you wish, Plato." Charity looked as though she might continue, but Kate clucked. "No, no. that's too much to have to live up to. Let them make their own names for themselves. Something solid and English would do just fine. Charles. Edward. Elizabeth."

Everyone threw out names, and Lucy watched June. She was like a mother to all of them, had taken on so much of their care for all those years. Lucy's heart filled with gratitude at the thought that she had none of those worries or cares any longer. Now, June looked happy and warm and ready to be a mother to her own children. And then move to Morley's estate.

Would Lucy lose all those most dear to her?

She shook her head.

Then Grace turned to her. "What's wrong, Lucy?"

Everyone stopped their giggling and laughing and looked at her.

"Are you well?" June reached a hand to touch her face how she'd always done. "She feels a little warm."

"I'm fine. I'm well, I'm just…" Her lip quivered, and to her dismay and shock, tears filled her eyes.

"Oh no!" Grace wrapped arms around her neck and shoulders. "What is it?"

Lucy laughed and her tears fell and she didn't even know

what to say. So many things had caused these tears, the good as well as the difficult.

"I'm just…" She tried to take a large breath, but it quivered in her chest as it entered and left. "I don't want to lose this."

They moved together in a large hug, all of them together how they used to do. And Lucy felt safe for a moment and, most importantly, loved.

"What has you worried all of a sudden?" Charity always overthought everything.

"Right at this moment, I had such a new and foreign thought overtake me I was quite surprised by it."

They leaned closer.

"And that thought was?" Charity dramatically waved her hand around.

"Well…" Lucy fidgeted like she hadn't since she'd banned the behavior years ago. "What if I don't have a love match, and no one in my household…loves me?" Her lips quivered again, and she didn't know what else to do but consider herself utterly silly. "What if I love all of you and we never see each other and I…" She closed her mouth. That was it. Seeing them all like this, and knowing she had never really sought for a love match, had all of a sudden caused a great loneliness to surface. One she hadn't felt or considered before.

June came around to where Lucy sat on the bed and then pulled her into a hug, a real tight big sister and mother hug. "Now, my dear Lucy. You may marry whoever you wish. You can marry for title as you've always claimed to want *and* for love. You may hurry into things or wait. It is totally up to you."

Lucy squeezed her back, letting her words sink into and comfort all the worried places in her heart. Could she really just marry whomever she pleased? An image of Mr. Sullivan laughing up into the sun suddenly burst into her mind, and she blinked him away just as quickly. *Not quite anyone.*

But June's words were comforting. She looked at them all. "And no matter whom we all marry, we must always make time for moments like this one."

"Agreed." Charity patted her shoulder. Which was about as touchy as Charity became. Except for their group hugs.

"Now, no more talk of leaving and marrying. Isn't it bad enough that Logan insisted on living in his own home?"

"At least they stayed in Brighton."

Grace's pout was really quite charming.

"But they both could have just as easily found rooms here at the castle."

They laughed and then moved on to discussing Charity's latest ideas for service. She'd been reading up on foundries. And the plight of these children chilled them all. Surely there was more they could do for the babies just left there. And then they drifted over to the latest colors in gowns, and they started talking about this next round of gowns for the season down in Brighton.

A servant knocked at the door.

"Yes, Timpson, what is it?" June waved him in closer.

"The Sullivans have left you with some of the greens from their gardens and this very fine pie." He held up the pie on a platter. "If I may, it is still warm."

"Oh, how lovely of them. Are they still here?"

"They are. The eldest son, Mr. Sullivan, dropped it off with his younger sister. I believe they are still in the drive."

"Invite them in, please. We shall taste of this pie with them."

"Sister!" Lucy was about to shake her head with her ready

complaint that they couldn't be seen as overly friendly with the servants, but she stopped. What did it matter? No one was about but the family. And the Sullivans were quite nice, especially one. "What a good and kind idea."

Everyone turned to her with mouths dropping to their chests.

"What? I think June is good to treat the servants well. They are people, after all. And it was good of them to bring us greens and a warm pie." She laughed. "Must you all stare at me so?"

"We just don't know what has become of the Lucy we once knew. But never you fear, sister, you may have a change of heart at any time you wish and we will allow you the grace to become something other than what you've always been."

"Goodness. I don't know that I'm ready to become anything at all. I just thought today, on my ride, how very kind and well-mannered Mr. Sullivan is as well as his family. So I find them the most deserving sorts of people."

"As do I." June nodded. "So, let us go greet our guests."

They filed out of June's room and made their way down the long hallway that overlooked the courtyard below. Lucy strained her eyes for a sight of Mr. Sullivan and his sister but realized that they might have already been shown into the front parlor which was not visible from the banister or courtyard area.

When they entered the front parlor, Mr. Sullivan and his sister stood.

He glanced in her direction once, quickly, nodded a half nod, and then turned to face the rest.

And that brief moment, that acknowledgement that they'd experienced something together, something more and separate from the rest of her sisters, gave Lucy such a thrill she had to grip the back of the nearest chair. Calming her breath, she smiled at them all, hoping not to be noticed.

But Grace called over, "Lucy, are you quite all right?" She looked at the rest of them and then back to Lucy. "She hasn't been the same since she returned from her ride."

At that, everyone turned to Mr. Sullivan, and Lucy about melted into the floor with the awkward moment that followed. She stammered out, "I am perfectly all right. My ride was lovely. The loveliest I've had…ever really." And then her cheeks flamed red. She could feel the heat overtake her face. "Oh dear, but I do think I should like some tea."

"Oh, certainly." June waved them closer to the seating arrangement near the fire. "We have asked that you join us in devouring this rather scrumptious-looking pie."

"Might we?" Margaret, Mr. Sullivan's younger sister, was probably two years younger than Grace but acted even younger still. Perhaps because she was the only girl, or perhaps because they all seemed to dote on her, Lucy couldn't be certain, but she was a lovely girl at any rate, almost as lovely as her brother.

She astounded herself with these thoughts. Perhaps all the talk of love and being free to marry and their earlier ride that was absolutely more intimate than it should have been addled her brain. But she was feeling much more comfortable and at ease with the Sullivans than she had before.

"And what flavor is this most delicious of gifts?" she surprised herself by asking.

Mr. Sullivan turned, and where he had previously let his sister answer most questions, he held her gaze. "This is a personal Sullivan favorite, from the berries in our own patch."

"Mulberry." Margaret stood taller. "With some blackberries to make it sweet."

"That sounds amazing." Lucy smiled. "Thank you for your kindness."

"It is our pleasure," Mr. Sullivan murmured. "Mum commanded us to bring this first one straight."

"She commanded me. And you insisted on coming." Margaret frowned. "You've never cared to make food deliveries before."

June looked from one to the other and at Lucy, and then she nodded. "And very good of him to, as I'm certain it's better you're not wandering the grounds by yourself, am I correct?"

"Quite so, Lady Morley." Mr. Sullivan's manners were impeccable as far as Lucy was concerned.

The servants brought in a tray with plates for all and another tray for the tea.

Soon, they all had a piece of pie on their laps, tea at their sides, and the warm glow of friendship extended between them.

Lucy felt the whole thing was as odd as it was provident. For how could such a connection with another, a servant no less, happen twice in one day, when it had never happened before previously?

She considered her words. Had it never happened? They entertained guests, even tenants, all the time. Morley and Gerald loved the Sullivans. They were known to consult on all manner of issues with them frequently, and Lucy may have even remembered the men in Morley's office, taking brandy.

She puzzled until Mr. Sullivan addressed her particularly. "And will you be staying here for the season as well?"

Lucy had not even been attending their conversation. "I believe so, yes."

He nodded. And then the conversation continued around them, but there seemed to be a new bubble between them two.

"I enjoy the Brighton season."

"Have you not ever wished to go to London?"

"I have…" She sighed. "But it seems so far and apart from the others." She shrugged. "Brighton has been sufficient."

"I'm happy to hear it. Perhaps we might continue working the horses?" He paled somewhat. "I apologize. That was…" He placed his cup and shifted as though he might leave, but she reached out.

"No. That was very kind. You noticed I have been in need of a good ride, and you too are in need of more exercise and training for the stallion. I appreciate your offer and attention to this detail. Perhaps I shall repeat the outing tomorrow?"

"Excellent." The gratitude in his eyes warmed her heart. He had no need to be concerned. A man as good and noble as he would not be trying to overstep the bounds of their stations. He was merely being attentive and kind.

They continued making conversation with the Sullivans as if they were old family friends. And when the hour grew later and they at last stood to go, Lucy felt that they were indeed family friends.

"Please send our love and gratitude to your dear mother. And your father as well." June's warmth as a hostess was to be greatly admired.

"We will, thank you." Mr. Sullivan bowed, and even Margaret performed a perfect curtsey.

"Thank you again."

They were shown out by servants, and the sisters were quiet for many minutes after they had left.

"Singularly lovely people," June said at last.

"I felt as if I was speaking to the friends of Morley that have come to call." Kate sipped her tea.

"Yes, that Mr. Sullivan is lovely. Isn't he?" Grace looked to Lucy. Which she found singularly disconcerting.

Lucy brushed off her dress. "I suppose they are tolerable."

The other sisters laughed.

"Oh, Lucy. Don't be putting on airs. They were as grand as any guests we ever had before June married Morley." Charity dismissed the whole topic with the wave of her hand.

"I'm not putting on airs. I'm just unsure why everyone must look at me for approval about our visit with the stable hand."

"Because you are the one most apt to disapprove, and yet you seemed so wholly approving." Grace giggled. "Did I hear you telling him you would be riding again tomorrow?"

Lucy commanded her features to remain passive. "Of course. As that is his job in our home. I found the ride exhilarating this morning and much needed, if you must know. And yes, their company was pleasant." She stood. "And now I think I shall at last finally take my bath, if you're all finished badgering me."

Their expressions of shock told Lucy that perhaps she'd read the situation all wrong but did little to give her any remorse whatsoever. She hoped rather for a sound escape.

Which she took in that moment.

And not a moment too soon, for the sounds of Morley and Logan laughing in the entryway told her the men had returned, and while she loved them dearly, she was not of a mind to continue to entertain.

The solitude of her room was welcome indeed. And once the servants began bringing in buckets of hot water, the anticipation of a lovely evening enveloped her while she waited for everything to be prepared. She sat at her chair and lifted a book into her lap while Susan started brushing through her hair at the very tips.

"Did the pins come out in your ride, miss?"

"Yes, they did." She considered her maid. They rarely spoke. Perhaps Lucy could be more like her sisters and converse with her maid. "I enjoyed it. But I do think it will be a bear to finally clear of knots."

"If you enjoyed it, may as well make a mess of things. You'll always have me to clean it up afterward."

Lucy smiled. That was the kindest, most tender comment she ever got out of Susan, and it warmed her toes. "Thank you."

"You're welcome, miss."

When the bath was at last ready, and she was thoroughly and completely clean, she sat back in the water for a moment, relaxing. What an eye-opening day she'd had. What an amazing eye-opening afternoon. Talking with the staff and their families was pleasant. Not that she ignored their staff. But she felt it was her place to ignore them. Didn't everyone else ignore their staff? And while all of that was true, and there were good reasons for not having to converse openly and freely all the time with the staff, it was also nice to feel like she had a bit of a pleasant relationship with Susan now. She'd try a bit more conversation with her tomorrow.

When she was dried and warmed with a warming pan and a large fire in her fireplace, she opened up a book again and attempted to read.

But all she could think about was Mr. Sullivan.

She wished to journal. There was no other way to sort through her thoughts. Lord Fellon, Mr. Sullivan, Lord Fellon, all competed in a crazy, disjointed jumble of thoughts which she couldn't understand. Why was Mr. Sullivan even in her thoughts? And how did he come to be competing for attention with the duke's son?

She arose from her desk and got out her inkwell and quill and her small journal and began to write.

Lord Fellon had asked her to dance for two sets last they'd been together. And he'd hovered.

People had talked.

But then he'd left Brighton and hadn't returned in over a fortnight.

The other lords were some she found amusing. Lord Kenworthy was more of a brooding type. And he seemed aware of her at least. He always asked her to dance. And perhaps gave deference to Lord Fellon when he was near. She considered them both. "Perhaps I should make a decision and show more pointed attention there?" This called for a list.

As she thought through her situation, many interruptions in the guise of Mr. Sullivan came to mind. His laugh, his smile, his easy nature, his determination to be proper with her, his desire to assist, his strength as he put her up on her horse, his jawline.

She stopped, wishing she could erase that last line. His jawline? But there it was. And he did have a marvelous jawline. Imagining him in a cravat would indeed be a worthy endeavor. She shook her head. If she were silly minded.

Which she wasn't, at all. And yet, here she was, thinking about Mr. Sullivan in a crisp cravat. What would he look like in breeches and jacket and hessians? She smiled.

And then she closed her journal even though the ink was still wet, a bit startled with her line of thought. But what more could she do? He was a handsome man. That knowledge was indisputable. But the fact that he was a stable hand had always negated the noticeability of his handsomeness. Until today.

And what had changed so much about today?

She had no answer. But she did know that she needed to get her head back on straight. Yes, June was correct. She could marry anyone she wanted. Certainly, they would all draw the line at servants. And she really did think she probably still wanted to be a duchess. Who wouldn't want to be a duchess? She thought about the men involved and knew she could easily fall in love with them as much as anyone else. Perhaps.

But would they love her back?

Her stomach tightened again, and she automatically began going through the lists of things in her deportment that must be in place in order for her to be the proper debutante. Her chin rose. Her ankles crossed. Her hands folded gently in her lap. Her mouth held a pleased expression, and her forehead relaxed. Surely, they would love someone as proper as she.

Then she opened her journal again, and she wrote all the finer qualities of the men who would be dukes.

And surprised herself with such little knowledge of them.

Before she went to sleep, she determined that she would indeed need to know them much better before she could make any kind of decision about their suitability.

And that thought right there was such a huge deviation from her previous fixation on title alone that she had to stare at the words in her journal for a minute more before they sank in appropriately.

Were she to guess, she would predict that even after knowing them better, she would still choose to marry a man who would be a duke. But the feeling of choice, the feeling of freedom was lovely, and she determined to explore this train of thought further.

She put away her quill and the inkwell and closed her journal. More to be thought about tomorrow, thoughts that would likely fill her days until the coming season began.

With Lord Fellon firmly in her mind in a dogged determination, she closed her eyes. But opened them immediately when his face was replaced by the man with chestnut curls, a ready grin, and a firm respect for her, standing out on the windy cliffs.

3

The sisters had decided that the next day would be a day to do some more exploring around the castle, especially while all of them were in town and staying at the castle for a couple days at least. They had opened up nearly all the rooms at last and were at this point going through some crates in one particular room that had been inaccessible earlier. But as the final touches were being made to walls and the opening of doors and floors, the last of the storage was cleared. And the sisters were determined to explore, with the hope that more information would be found as to their ancestors and their connection to William the Conqueror.

Morley, Gerald, and Logan had all joined them. Everyone sat in front of one crate or another. Morley leaned back from his digging through old parchments. "So, let's review what we know so far."

June nodded. "I agree. This all started with the discovery of a remarkable set of jewels." She smiled.

"Which turned out to be a gorgeous wedding gift for June." Kate smiled approvingly.

June raised a hand to her neck. The jewels were obviously locked away, but the gesture was a pretty one. "With plenty of jewels left for settings for you all."

"And a letter from William himself, if you were to ask me, that's the best part." Charity shifted in her seat. "I'm itching to unroll some of these parchments." In the box in front of her looked to be some old writings. "Even though I know they could not themselves read and write, they had to have dictated to scribes. These might contain their thoughts if not their own hand."

"More recent generations could obviously read and write." Lucy was as intrigued as anyone.

"But what do we know about their origins? The letter said, 'I, William, Duke of Normandy, do hereby bequeath this land and castle to the Molyneux family, my most loyal general, and to his descendants from this time and forever. The jewels in this chest are gifts for his daughters and their daughters and so on, through time. May you care for this bequeathal and keep it for generations to come.'" June had it memorized.

"Have you been giving this some thought, June?" Lucy was impressed.

"Some. I do think it is remarkable how William desired that the castle stay in his family, that he wished the jewels to bless the women descendants, and that they have fallen into our hands seemingly by chance. The castle certainly has stayed with the family line, but the ability to actually live here, to be renovating, to find the jewels in the first place, all relied upon the spoils of a card game." June shook her head.

Gerald shook his head. "No, cousin." He grinned. "Even though our familial connection might be distant, I think of you that way, as a true cousin. And remember, I was fixing the place up and would have continued whether or not Morley became involved. He became a part of the story so he could meet you." Gerald nodded in June's direction.

"And what a blessing that has been." Morley lifted June's hand to his mouth. "One that increases my happiness every day."

Charity smiled at them both but then waved her hand. "And the topic we are discussing, which is solving the mystery of the remaining pieces of this castle and our place in the line. This is why we are here, no doubt."

"True. What else do we know so far?" Lucy looked to Logan.

"Wait. There is more we know before Logan joined us." Gerald looked to be enjoying this as much as any of them. "The use of your father's Standish seal on the letter, the gift from William to his brother, shows the care he hoped to offer the Molyneaux family."

"And we have a rattle, if you recall, with the initials of the daughter MMM, the daughter who came to live here." They all turned to Logan. He grinned. "In our library, we discovered that she spent much of her time here. And that many did not know of her existence during her time. Or if they did, it was not spoken of." Logan and Kate shared a glance. "Perhaps she was not of noble birth."

And this is where Amelia piped up, "Which is perfectly acceptable."

"Naturally." Gerald and Amelia shared such a look of love that Lucy's hunger for such a relationship simmered inside. Amelia as a shop owner had discovered her relations to a baron. But her father had been a commoner. They had escaped the ton to live out their days in happiness without such passing judgment on them and their children. Though Amelia had relations to a well-respected baron, she considered herself to be commoner more than anything, now duchess of course. Their story was more romantic than any Lucy had heard. And the love they shared gave evidence to their commitment every day.

"So what more do we know?" Logan looked from one to the other.

Lucy laughed. "Nothing, but we had a lot of clues to a lot of things. Logan's books are particularly helpful, I think."

"My history books confirm what you have with these personal papers. William commissioned this castle be built. His wife refused to live here except for a short time in their lives. And then it looks to me as though a daughter continued on. Looks as though she valued her father's position in England and disapproved of her mother's refusal to come support him. The daughter could read and write. She might have had questionable heritage. But she might not. And she certainly kept to herself. But there were hints of descendants from her as well." Logan shifted. "The brother, the Molyneaux line, is revered here and in France. What the books show also is how many of the English royalty are all descended from William or his family. Nearly everyone. Which puts you in noble company and relations."

"And it was the intent of William that the castle remain with his daughters," Lucy pointed out. That part of the story always warmed her. A man, somewhere in their family line, had made particular care and provision for the women, for her by proxy.

Logan nodded. "We should convene in our library tomorrow to see if there are any more clues."

They all quieted at that, studying the remaining trunks and piles of things around them.

Lucy wandered through the other items still to be discovered. She knelt beside what was perhaps a large rug, rolled up from a pile in the corner. "What is this?"

"They pulled some of those things from an old attic that is now gone and part of the east tower," Morley called over to her from across the room. "Anything interesting?"

She peered inside, pulling years of debris off the top. "Looks like an old tapestry. Someone want to help me unroll it?"

Morley helped lift it and carry it over by the light from a window, and they unrolled it along the floor.

Lucy leaned closer. "I can't make it out." She stepped back to get a bigger view. "Oh! I think it's a tree?"

Morley traced lines with his finger. "More like a tapestry with the family line. See here. That's a name, and another. These are all the branches of the family."

The diagram in the tapestry looked very much like an actual tree. But Morley was correct. Now that he pointed it out, the fabric was full of names.

"There might be hundreds of them." Kate gasped. "Whose family is this?"

And Lucy knew that each one of them hoped it was somehow their family.

"Do you see the Molyneaux family? Or William himself?" Grace had been particularly hopeful that they could claim a relation. "Or Standish?"

Gerald called from the other side of the room, "You know, if you are related, and I'm related, that makes us…"

"Related." Grace laughed. "But I already feel like you and Amelia are family."

"And happy we are to hear it. Our young lads need good role models to look up to."

Morley started to roll it back up. "We must have better lighting. And a flat surface. Let's move this to the dining table."

"Absolutely. That table can hold anything. It is huge." June's excitement spread to them all.

He lifted it up on a shoulder and carried it with everyone following to the main dining room. A servant approached.

"We need a well-lit room. Could you have extra lamps and candles brought to the dining room?"

"Yes, my lord."

Gerald laughed. "We are an impatient bunch."

"Of course. This tapestry could have the key to the mystery we are trying to solve." Lucy hurried after them, hardly breathing or holding her breath alternately.

"And what mystery is that?" Gerald chuckled. "To prove that these lovely women are of noble blood?"

No one answered.

"Because I don't need a tapestry to tell me that. You are special indeed." He held his Amelia closer.

June rested a hand on his arm. "Thank you, Gerald. You have been special to me since that first day I met you."

He shuddered. "On my way to deposit a Lady Rochester in her new home, may she rest in peace."

After an attempted relationship with her footman, the two ran off together toward Scotland but got in a carriage accident on the way. Gerald shook his head. "Naturally, I do not wish to speak ill of the dead, but she did attempt to marry me under the false pretense of caring for my estate while she truly loved the footman."

"Oh dear." Lucy felt a small thread of discomfort during

this conversation. A twinge of guilt that she had entered any mode of familiarity with a servant. Was she to be like Lady Rochester?

"Speaking of servants, we had the Sullivans over for tea and the most delicious pie today." June smiled at Lucy as if she read her mind.

"Did you?" Gerald nodded. "Excellent family. We are hanging onto them by their coattails here at the castle."

"What do you mean?" Lucy helped unroll the tapestry on the table.

"Well, men come from all over to consult with Mr. Sullivan the father on which horses to buy and with Mr. Sullivan the son on how to train them. The prince himself has his eye on the family to come work at his stables at the Royal Pavilion."

"No!" Lucy interjected without thinking and then had no idea how to explain herself. But no one seemed to notice anything odd in her comment.

"It's difficult to believe that we are to be so sought after here, but we truly do have an excellent establishment, and once this castle is all the way complete, we will have one of the finer homes in the area certainly, in all of England as well." Gerald stood taller. "I'm quite proud of it."

"As am I. Best win at a game of cards I've ever had." Morley wrapped his arm around June. And they shared a small smile.

Lucy loved their relationship. The love between them was obvious, and she was grateful for it every day.

Gerald and Amelia also shared a similar love. And Lucy had never heard the whole story, but something about Amelia being a tea shop owner when Gerald met her intrigued Lucy.

When the servants had filled the room with light, they

each leaned over the tapestry and circled it, trying to make sense of it all.

Lucy pointed to the top. "So that is the start of these generations there." She fingered the fabric. "And this is not so very old. I wonder if someone nearer to our time made it and added the names?"

June shook her head. "No, see here. It's in excellent shape, but the tapestry itself is very old." The fabric underneath was fading and yellow, and the edges were fraying.

Lucy studied the name at the top. It was faded. It ran together somewhat. But it clearly said Molyneaux.

And then next to him, starting his own whole line of descendants, was William's name. She traced her finger down name after name, generation after generation. And two generations down, the lines came together. "See, here is where the families intersect. This marriage right here." She peered closer. "But this is interesting. See. O'Sullivan. They brought in Irish blood? And…" She frowned. "The line ends."

Logan leaned closer. "I saw information about O'Sullivans. Found it interesting to see the Irish there, so it stood out to me. Might be a more complete history and some interesting scandal?" Logan wiggled his eyebrows.

"Oh? Perhaps that's why the line stops? Someone didn't wish it to continue?"

"That is so sad. It's not as though you can erase your family." Lucy frowned.

"But if they were an embarrassment to the line? If they weren't worthy to inherit? There are lots of reasons to exclude them legally, I suppose." Gerald looked thoughtful.

Everyone gathered in closer to see over Lucy's shoulder. "But the intercepted lines continue. See here." She traced the Molyneaux down through the generations. They leaned closer.

Until she saw names she recognized. "There's Great-grandfather." She squealed. "Reginald Standish."

The letters were stitched and the threading coming loose in many places. But his name, clear as any, was stitched into the fabric.

"This last entry could not have been too long ago. I mean, someone who at least knew of Great-grandfather."

"And then what? Threw the tapestry in the rubbish here at the castle?" Charity shook her head, but the excitement on her face was obvious.

June held a hand to her mouth in thought. "And the mystery continues. But here it is, in yet another place, proof of our relations to them. The Molyneux and William lines connect to give us Great-grandfather's place in this history."

The group was quiet for a moment.

"And so we wish to learn what has happened since the time of your great-grandfather."

"I hope we want to know." Lucy held her hands together. "It can't have been good to bring such poverty and obscurity on us all."

"Or sometimes, things happen that have nothing to do with such things as good or not good, just perhaps unlucky?" Morley was ever the optimist. "Take this castle. It might just be that the whole of this side of the family came into hard times."

"Let us hope it is something akin to bad luck." Gerald and Morley shared a look, and Lucy was grateful for their friendship.

"And with so much evidence that the luck has turned, we might celebrate." Grace's contagious smile lifted them all.

"Certainly." Gerald grinned.

"I wonder if there is more information in some of those

scrolls." Charity linked arms with Kate. "Shall we return for just a bit more?"

They groaned in response.

And Morley raised his hands. "How about we instead head outside for a picnic? Or a meal in the courtyard? The weather is lovely, and all this research is making me hungry."

"I as well." June smiled.

And it was decided. The group convened in the courtyard. Servants brought out chairs and smaller tables. And the repast they shared was some of the castle's delicious fare.

Gerald nodded in approval. "You have hired an additional chef."

"From France." Morley grinned. "We have some of the finest meals in the finest location in such a renowned place full of history. I may never wish to leave."

"Will you be returning to your estate any time soon?" Gerald looked as though he hesitated to ask.

But Morley turned his attention to each one of the sisters. "We would like to make the bulk of our living here, but the Morley estate, it has need of its master. And the tenants want to meet its heir. So we will indeed begin travel between the two once the child is old enough and June feels well enough."

A heavy sort of melancholy settled over the group. In truth, they would have to expect that they would separate, but seeing it happen right before their eyes was another thing altogether.

Kate reached for Logan's hand. "We too will be heading back to London for the season. Lord Dennison here has another bill to see through to its success."

4

T he next morning found Lucy and their whole party together on their way to the stables. It had been decided that there would be a family ride in place of Lucy's normal solitary ride. She hid her disappointment that she wouldn't be able to spend another quiet morning with Mr. Sullivan, but it was likely for the best. Time alone with the handsome stable hand was perhaps not advisable.

Grace clung to one of her arms and Kate the other. "This is the best of all days, with all of us together like this."

Lucy grinned at them both.

"I agree." Charity's words from just in front of them while she walked with June made Lucy even more happy. Charity was busy all the time, planning things, doing things, writing things; rarely did she make time or care for the more frivolous things in life, which included, apparently, marrying. To hear her sister express such a sentiment comforted Lucy somewhat. She knew her sister loved them, but it was nice to also know that she wanted to be with them. Sometimes, Lucy's own silly insecurities, though very real, were also perhaps not founded on anything true.

The stables were a row of several large buildings, well kept, newly painted, fences mended. They were perhaps the part of the castle grounds that never had need of huge repairs. Lucy suspected they had the Sullivans to thank for that careful attention.

As they approached, the sounds of a carriage reached them, and Morley and Gerald made a step to go back toward the house. "Who do you suppose needs greeting?"

But the carriage continued past the castle, and when it came into view, Grace gasped. "It's the royal crest."

Lucy gripped Kate's arm. Luckily, she was perfectly presentable in her riding habit. "Is it the prince?"

"Coming around behind the castle? Surely not." Gerald shook his head.

"Oh, true. Then what on earth is this about?"

The carriage pulled to a stop in front of the stables, to their side.

And to Lucy's complete amazement, Mr. Sullivan, father and son, stepped out. They smiled, warm, engaging, Sullivan-matching smiles, and bowed deeply.

Gerald stepped forward. "Mr. Sullivan, Mr. Sullivan. Good to see you both."

Lord Morley reached his hand out to clasp both men's. "Any news from the Royal Pavilion?"

The carriage pulled forward and turned around on the drive up ahead.

The two men exchanged glances. Lucy watched attentively to see if she could discern anything from the younger Mr. Sullivan. His gaze did flicker in her direction briefly. But other than that, nothing of note seemed different. She could do nothing but stare. A cravat, hessians, breeches—her Mr. Sullivan looked better than she'd ever dared to suppose in such a look.

Then Mr. Sullivan gestured to the stables. "Perhaps some of you would like to meet in our office to discuss the most recent news?" He seemed perfectly deferential as always, but there was an element of esteem about him, something Lucy couldn't quite put her finger on but that it seemed to give the man a more equal footing perhaps in their conversations?

Morley nodded. "Certainly. We are about to take a ride, but I believe all of us would be most interested in news, and then we can take out the horses after." He looked around, and at ready nods from every person in their party, Mr. Sullivan nodded and then gestured that they should continue.

Mr. Conor Sullivan lingered a moment so that he came to stand with the sisters. Lucy leaned forward across Grace at her side. "What news?"

He laughed. "I think my father wishes to share it from his office."

Grace frowned. "But we are not good at being patient when news is involved." Her pout was charming.

And Mr. Conor Sullivan laughed yet again. "I am at the disposal of others. But it was intriguing news indeed."

"Oh, and of course, he has to raise our curiosity even further." Grace smiled.

Mr. Conor Sullivan held his hand out, indicating the office door. "And see? We have arrived. The news shall be divulged in but a few more brief moments." He waited to allow them all to enter first, and then they made their way into the rather small office space.

When it was obvious that only a portion of their group would fit at all comfortably inside, Mr. Sullivan stepped back out and stood at their front. "I'm pleased at the timing of our meeting today, for I would greatly appreciate your thoughts on a most recent development."

Lucy moved to stand beside Mr. Sullivan the younger. "Good news or bad?" She spoke under her breath, not able to wait.

"I don't know." He faced his father, but with his lowered voice, she knew his response was meant just for her.

"Are you well?"

"I don't know." One corner of his mouth ticked up.

When she was about to ask another question, he turned to her. "I believe all is about to be revealed." His eyes widened, and with a teasing smile, he looked once again at his father.

Her huff of air in response tugged a greater smile from him.

His father had finished thanking them all for being there and for their constant magnanimous support over the years, etc.

Then he cleared his throat. "As you may know, in addition to serving the needs of the castle stables for generations, our family is also sought after from time to time in an advisory role."

Morley laughed. "You are being modest. Everyone comes to you first before buying a single bit of horseflesh."

"And to my son when considering training one."

Lucy looked up at Mr. Sullivan in surprise. "I didn't know you were quite so renowned."

He tipped his head to her.

Then his father continued. "It might also not be a secret that the prince has been one of those who consults with us."

Mr. Conor Sullivan stiffened beside her. Interesting. Did he not relish the pending news?

"Today, he has summoned us to his palace and asked, or rather requested, that we consider furthering these same positions in his own royal stables."

Lucy gasped.

Beside her, Mr. Conor Sullivan's gaze dropped to his boots.

No one spoke for many minutes.

But finally, Morley held out his hand. "Congratulations. You will be greatly missed, I can assure you of that."

But Mr. Sullivan shook his head. "We haven't yet given our response."

Gerald's mouth might have dropped to the earth. "But surely, man, this is not something you refuse? Denying the prince anything is not advisable. And accepting would surely be most profitable."

Mr. Sullivan nodded. "Perhaps. But be assured, he was most generous in his praise and expressed a great understanding about our possible desire to stay where our family has been for many generations. In fact, he alluded to information most intriguing to me, as though our family connection to the castle were stronger than I know it to be."

Lucy nodded. She well understood that sentiment.

"The stables have been in better condition than the castle all these years." Gerald smiled. "Your efforts have obviously not gone unnoticed." He clapped Mr. Sullivan on the shoulder. "By us either."

June nodded beside Morley. "We'd be a mess, worse than we were, without such a well-organized and kept-up stables."

Morley seemed to be thinking greatly. "And what can we do to assist in your decisions?"

They talked of options and benefits of staying at the castle or moving on to work with the prince, and Lucy quickly became bored with the lot of it. She drifted over to the horses' stalls.

Firestone had stuck her nose over the edge, and Lucy was itching to rub her down. She reached for a brush out of the side bucket and brushed it along her neck and upper back.

"She's a beautiful horse."

Young Mr. Conor Sullivan's closeness surprised her, but she took it in stride and continued to brush down the horse.

"She is. And as daring on the inside as she is pretty on the outside, but you saw some of that."

"Determined to win." He nodded. "Should we get her saddled up for you?"

Lucy looked back at their group, and the conversation seemed more focused, more determined, and to capture more attention from the remaining participants. Which included Gerald, Morley, Charity, June, and Mr. Sullivan.

"Perhaps we could saddle up three? For us and you?"

His eyebrows rose in pleasure, but he just nodded.

"I can saddle mine."

He sized her up. That's the best way she could describe the feeling of his gaze going from her boots to the top of her head, and then he nodded. "Can ye now?"

"As you know, thank you very much."

"Well, then let's be seeing you do it." His challenge settled in right where all pleasurable things go in her mind, and she let the juiciness of it flow around inside while she turned from him to head to the tack room.

She grabbed a saddle blanket and then lifted the saddle. It was heavier than she remembered but otherwise manageable. She made her way to Firestone while Mr. Sullivan was saddling up Grace's pony.

But she knew he saw her. And she hoped he was

impressed when she lifted the whole of it up on Firestone's back, where she adjusted it to fit just right and then tightened the straps. Showing off a bit for Mr. Sullivan, a known expert with horses, brought more enjoyment than it should have.

The others had finished their discussion and were ready to join them on horses, so Mr. Sullivan the elder and younger were busy getting saddles ready, though the other servants could have taken care just as easily.

When it came time to mount, no mounting blocks were in sight. Though she looked at Mr. Conor Sullivan in suspicion, he merely approached Grace. "Would you like assistance?"

"Oh yes, thank you."

His hands went around her waist, and she was up on the horse in one motion.

Charity called over, "I don't want to offend some of our sensibilities and hoist my leg all the way up in the stirrup, could you assist me as well?"

"Certainly, miss." Mr. Sullivan dipped his head, and within moments, Charity was up on her horse as well.

He turned to Lucy. And a rumble of anticipation hummed through her. His steps were slow, or perhaps they seemed so.

When her eyes met his, he delayed averting his gaze just long enough for her rumble to turn to new heightened awareness. She placed her hands on his shoulders. An earthy smell of outdoors, pine, leather, and the tiniest bit of hay filled the air around him. And his cravat...he was everything she'd hoped he might appear in a cravat. She swallowed. As his fingers circled her waist, he lifted her slowly up onto the saddle. She adjusted her skirts, not daring to meet his gaze again. But he placed his hand on Firestone. So she lifted her lashes.

"I wonder if we might converse."

No one was paying them any attention.

"Certainly."

"I find I am in need of your advice."

She nodded. "I shall do my best to be of assistance, certainly."

With an extra amount of attention to Firestone, he let his hand linger close on her horse's flank for a moment more, and then he turned to mount his own horse.

Her breath left in a woosh. And nothing she did would make her hands sit still. They touched her bonnet, her reins, then clutched together. She shifted her weight.

Firestone obviously noticed her anticipation and danced in place.

"Whoa, girl." Lucy reached forward to pat her side. Right where Mr. Sullivan had touched her. She jerked her hand away.

Firestone shuffled in the small space.

Mr. Conor Sullivan turned to her in concern. And without speaking, he stepped back to let her go out first.

And even their silent communication sent waves of unsettlement through her, a pleasing sensation but alarming as well.

But as soon as she was out in the air, the crisp feel to things, the open sky, she felt a bit of herself returning. And thank the stars for that. Curiosity about one stable hand or even a secret lingering thought about him were one thing, openly flushed cheeks and girlish reactions to him were something else entirely and must not be noticed by him or any of the others.

She kept Firestone in check like she should herself until the horse whinnied, and then she loosened the reins. "Sorry, girl. Let's show them what we can do."

The mare didn't need to be told twice. She leapt forward and tore out across the pasture.

Voices called out behind her, but she ignored them, filled with an urge to run, to be as far from the beguiling presence of Mr. Sullivan as possible.

5

Firestone sensed her urgency, and she tore off faster than Lucy had seen her run. She raced for the back part of the property. The line that followed the edge of the woods. Did she want to hide? No, that was ridiculous, but in a crazy back corner of her mind, the idea was appealing. She tore over hedges, Firestone taking them in stride. The wind whipped across her face. But her bonnet stayed firmly attached. Susan had gone to great lengths to prevent another hair situation like the one she had before.

Hooves sounded behind her, and she wasn't at all surprised when Mr. Conor Sullivan rode up beside her. His horse seemed to be straining. He wasn't on Devil's Nape this time. So she eased back on Firestone, and the mare moved gradually to an easy canter. Still fast. Still too quick to speak, which was exactly what Lucy wanted right now.

Mr. Sullivan didn't seem to mind or didn't say anything if he did. He merely rode out beside her with his face forward, watching the terrain.

The ground turned rocky, and with reluctance, Lucy

slowed them way down to a walk. "Easy girl. There. Easy now."

With her chin up, drinking in each breath of clean air, the sky stretched out around her, she felt a rising fire of independence inside. And a new confidence. She turned to Mr. Sullivan, unsure what she planned to say but determined to not be affected by him.

But his eyes cut her back to a vulnerable mess of a human. They were open, sincere, and full of emotion. He was hurting.

"What is it?"

"I've made things difficult for you. I'm sorry."

How did she respond to that statement? Yes. He'd made things difficult. Did he know in what manner? Had he made assumptions he should not be making? She studied the open vulnerability on his face that he had let her see, and she could do nothing but acknowledge his honesty and recognize the truth of his words.

Inside.

She could not breathe a word of the depth of her discomfort from her lips. Instead of responding at all, she tried to relax. "Well, we can have that conversation you wished to have." She shrugged.

"True." He turned his horse. "But shall we turn back? The ground here isn't good for the horses."

"Of course."

He rode close to her. The breeze was light. The sun warm. And if not for the distorted mess of emotion that flowed through her at an alarming rate, she would have felt quite at ease. Or as comfortable as she ever felt with Mr. Sullivan.

"The prince offered us a position in his palace."

She nodded. "I assumed as much."

"But we don't want to take it."

Somehow, she sensed this hesitance earlier. His father had said as much when he suggested they were thinking it over.

"Why?"

"The answer to that question is complicated and would be different depending on which Sullivan you asked."

She waited.

He didn't seem anxious to talk, but somehow, she knew he was formulating his next words carefully.

At last, he sighed. "The simple answer? I prefer having our own thing. For years, I've wanted to expand, to create a business. To breed, to train, to…I don't know, to become something more, something…" The eyes that stared into hers said so much more than his mouth. He wanted to rise above his station. He was reaching, like she was, for something more elevated in his life.

"And isn't working for the prince a definite rise in elevation?"

"It is. But would we ever leave? Would that consume our lives and become our everything?"

She considered him. And she knew what she should say. She should encourage him to take the job. Being a royal stablemaster was the highest form his job could take. There was nothing better than that for him. Unless he did in fact own his own establishment, but even then, a stable hand in the royal household might be a better opportunity, surely ensure improved clientele.

"Could you not perhaps do both?"

"Perhaps. Father suggests that above all things."

"What did you need my particular thoughts for?" She wondered what she could have to offer in such a conversation.

"In your dealings with the noble classes." He paused as if tasting his next words before he spoke them. "Have you seen any evidence of one person…rising in class to another, and there not being significant repercussions on that person or the family?" His gaze was turned away from her. She couldn't see how deeply he wanted to hear something positive in her response. And she didn't know what to say. Yes, she was close to a situation similar to what he described, Amelia and Gerald, but the other person in that duo was a duke. And they could be forgiven for many a thing. Also, Amelia might have started as a shop owner's daughter, but her mother was of noble blood. The ton were unforgiving in many instances that regarded the class of people. She knew. Oh, she knew having felt the years of mock pity and the charity from others who recognized their noble relations but were not willing to consider them equals due to their poverty.

"I'm not sure how to respond."

He nodded, his jaw tight.

"I do know people who have broken that class barrier. But there are always circumstances, always partial connections to the nobility. That kind of thing."

"One thing I fear." His voice came out hurried, almost gruff. "I fear that in working at the palace, I will so firmly place myself in servant class status that I will never recover."

"And here?"

"Here. We worked for so many years on our own, so much of our time being considered…independent. I think there is that understanding among some in the merchant classes. Some might even view us as a form of landowner?" His voice sounded almost pleading. "Or at least a business owner already."

She opened her mouth.

"We have only really ever served a family when yours arrived."

She prepared to respond, never having considered their situation in quite that way.

But a gunshot fired.

Her horse stumbled. Mr. Sullivan's reared back. He ducked and clung to his horse's mane. "Duck. Ride!"

She searched the forest and the area all around.

"Go!"

She hugged Firestone and urged her to race.

When Mr. Sullivan didn't join her, she whipped her head around and screamed when she saw him heading into the forest at top speed.

She turned immediately and raced after him, her thoughts screaming at her to stop at once but her heart knowing she could not leave a man to fight whatever danger lurked inside that forest alone.

Her body lay almost flat against Firestone as they made their way to the entry point in the forest she had seen him take.

They slowed to a walk and then a stop as she peered into the darkness caused by the dense foliage.

A gun fired again, and she screamed.

"Lucy! Go!" Mr. Sullivan tore through the trees toward the sound.

And Lucy waited, clenching her hands together, peering in through the trees.

But she heard nothing for what felt like a long time.

Then another gunshot rang through the trees, further away, and she realized the futility of her decision. She whipped her horse around and tore out back onto the meadow. She must find some help. She must send someone back in there after Mr. Sullivan. She must make sure he was all right.

That last gunshot had left such an eerie silence in its wake.

She raced across the meadow, back toward the house. Curse her initial ride that led her so far.

But shortly, over a ridge, two horses riding as fast as she headed her way.

Servants from the house. As soon as they stopped in front of her, she shouted, "Go! Gunshots in the woods. Mr. Sullivan went after, but I haven't seen him return."

They kicked into their horses and tore in the direction she pointed.

Morley and Gerald came soon after. They pulled to a stop almost on top of her, faces stricken with worry lines. "Are you all right?"

"Yes, yes, I'm fine, but Mr. Sullivan. He went after their gunshots. I heard another. And nothing. Please. We have to save him."

They followed her gaze to the forest. "We will send more servants directly." Morley's response was as expected. He looked concerned. He would do what he could, but Lucy was struck that he didn't immediately chase after him himself. And she knew he would be ridiculous to do so. But at the same time, she had done exactly that.

Her shoulders slumped. "He told me to ride, to go. I left him." Guilt filled her.

"As you should," Gerald said. "He did exactly as he should have done. Now come. I'll ride with you. And Morley here will race back to call for more servants."

She nodded. And Morley did just that.

The duke said little to her as they made their way, side by side, to the house. But after a moment, he cleared his throat. "I can't help but notice a particular…intensity between you and young Mr. Sullivan."

She gasped. "How could you notice such a thing?"

He laughed. "Well, now. I don't think anyone else but Amelia would have seen it. But it is there, isn't it?"

"Yes, but it's the silliest thing. New. Nothing has been said or done."

"But when you tore out of the barn, he raced after you. Before Morley or I could even think to be concerned."

She nodded.

"You have no understanding?"

"No! Of course not. Precious few words have even been spoken between us."

"Sometimes, these things happen, made more enticing by the forbidden nature of it."

"You and Amelia?"

He shook his head. "Nothing like that happened with us. She was more right than forbidden, as if the very breath we breathe was pulling us together."

Lucy considered his words up against her experience with Mr. Sullivan. A great confusion warred up inside. "But I'm not considering a single thing with him, nothing. I went on a ride. We talked a moment. The gunshots."

"He helped you up on your horse."

Her eyes shot to his, and she cursed his amusement.

"That one act has caused more trouble amongst people than any other. It's so…personal."

She nodded.

"And you have your own plans, do you not? Your cap set on Lord Fellon?"

"Yes."

"And he is interested?"

"I believe so."

"Then it is folly to consider this current little mishap of

emotion. The human heart sometimes surges with ridiculous notions. You must toss it aside as the thing it is."

"Of course, you are right. I cannot feel at ease until I do so."

"Excellent. And we will say no more of it."

"Thank you. The others must never know."

"You have my word."

They made their way across the grassland, and Lucy felt a semblance of relief regarding her situation. But she could not feel at ease fully until she knew that Mr. Sullivan was indeed well. "You don't think he was shot, do you?"

"I have no way of knowing. But I do know him to be a sensible sort of person, one of the most sensible of my acquaintance. Of a truth, if he wasn't so decidedly below your station, I would give a hearty approval..."

"Gerald."

"Apologies. I know that isn't helpful. Your heir to a dukedom will give you generations' worth of security. And that is worth something, to be sure."

His words sounded flat to her ears, and some of the previous ease he had created drained away, but she turned her head to the path in front and lifted her chin and pressed her lips together. "To be certain. I have felt the fear of an unsure path ahead. Were it not for you inheriting our fate, we should have died spinsters." The words came out in a rush. But they had been a certain terrible fear for so much of her young life that to say them, to face them head on, still brought back some of that concern.

"And I do believe fate was smiling on you all those years. You've been taken care of, have you not?"

"Certainly. I am grateful for all that has been done on our behalf. But it is not the same as knowing that you will always have food, clothes, education, comfort, for the entirety of your life. That is not something that is cheaply bought."

He said nothing more, but she knew Gerald. She knew he cared deeply for them and that he'd given up a considerable amount of his fortune seeing to their care. And brought them his best friend for June. He was dear indeed.

A group of horses rode toward them from the house. When they were close enough, Lucy saw that they were armed.

6

Lucy clutched at her reins the remaining ride back to the house. Nothing could ease her concern, nothing, until she had news of Mr. Sullivan's safety.

And then she was going to try and never see the man again.

Because this emotional upheaval that plagued the beating of her heart was too much for her ordered world. If this is what it meant when her heart was engaged, she had no space for it, except for those she already loved. She wished instead for the carefully planned and plotted marriage to a man who would be a duke. They could manage well together and never again would she be so agitated.

As soon as they were close enough to the castle, her sisters ran across the grass to meet her.

"I'll take your horse." Gerald reached for her reins as she slid to the earth.

Her feet brought her in great racing steps to the arms of her family. They encircled her, arms around each other, the five crying and hugging.

June's voice over all crooned, "I'm so grateful you are well."

"We heard the guns." Grace trembled beside her.

"I am well. I am perfectly well."

Their hug lasted for many moments, and then with Grace on one arm and Kate on the other, they made their way back up toward the castle.

"But Mr. Sullivan." She frowned to hide the quivering of her lip. "He... He rode in without thought, straight toward the sound of the guns."

"Oh, he is too good." June covered her face with her hand, and the others looked sufficiently concerned to appease Lucy's heart. Perhaps she was like every other caring female and had no special inclinations toward anyone. Perhaps Gerald was seeing things from his own imagination.

"I shall not sit easy until he is found." She clutched at her sisters' hands.

"Nor shall any of us. What a dear, dear family." Grace nodded.

Soon they were sitting by the fire, tea in hand and with a valiant attempt to distract themselves in their laps.

But the book in her hands went unread. The needlepoint in June's was not improved upon. No card was played, nor were any of the other distractions given much mind.

When at last Morley stepped into their parlor, waving off a footman's announcement, they rushed to their feet and were at his side in an instant.

"He is fine."

Their collective exhale brought on some relieved laughter.

Lucy felt she well and truly might faint, but she gripped Grace's arm and focused on Morley's face to hear his next words.

"Poachers. Apparently, the shots were never aimed at you, Lucy. But they could have found their mark regardless."

June gasped and clutched at the lace on the front of her dress.

Charity's arms went around her, and Morley said, "Come, sit. Let us discuss this by the fire."

When June was situated at his side, he continued. "The poachers have been caught and guards placed around the property. It will only take a few days of strict watching before the message will be sent. We do not welcome them on our land."

Lucy nodded. "And Mr. Sullivan? How did this come about?"

"Yes, Lucy said he raced straight toward the sound of gunfire." Grace's eyes glowed with appreciation.

"I didn't hear that part of the story. I suspect his version toned down some of his heroics." Morley winked. "But he did say that when the poachers noticed they were caught, they took off running, shot their gun into the air, and then continued."

Lucy gasped.

And the others looked equally worried.

"We shall never ever be able to fully repay him for saving our Lucy." June's face looked whiter than it should.

"Oh, June. I'm so sorry to have worried you."

"Of course, Lucy, and it certainly wasn't your fault we had these men with guns lurking about."

Morley nodded with an arm placed tighter around his wife. "Yes, we owe him a great debt, and with them considering leaving for the prince, perhaps it would behoove us to… have them for dinner?"

"Dinner?" June and Morley shared a long look, and then

she nodded. "Yes, I see, perhaps a casual dinner so as not to set them ill at ease."

"A casual dinner?" Lucy wondered a bit at the necessity to call it casual? Was she affronted in their behalf? Another reason to separate herself from them.

"Yes, you know, dressed in our day dresses, a simpler fare."

Lucy nodded. "They were wearing cravats to the prince's."

"Were they?" June frowned. "I didn't notice. Well, that's encouraging. Perhaps they won't feel as out of place as I thought."

Lucy wished it to be so. For even though she'd vowed to not be in his presence ever again, she wanted for him to feel at ease with her family. Perhaps she would get a tray in her room on the day they would come.

A servant stood at the entrance to the room with a letter tray in hand.

"Oh, Frederick, please come in."

"I have an express for Miss Lucy." He bowed.

Morley took the letter. "From the Duchess of Sussex? Their seal marks this parchment." With eyebrows up to his hairline, he handed Lucy the letter.

Everyone watched while she broke the seal.

She opened the paper and began to read out loud.

Dear Miss Lucy,

It has come to my attention that you have not as yet had a season in London. While Brighton has its diversions and has attracted a great many of the ton's eligible bachelors, nothing could replace the opportunity to experience a London season, and with me as your sponsor, no door will be shut to you.

Am I correct in assuming you are still interested in a

certain lord? Come. All expenses paid by me. We must get you in to the modiste by month's end.

And bring your sister Charity. This opportunity will have little use for her until she changes her bluestocking ways, but she will be a good companion to you and amusing for me.

Yours, etc.

Charity snorted. "Is it my purpose in life to amuse the old biddy?"

"Sister. Really."

"You can't blame me. What kind of invitation is that if you consider my perspective?"

"Too true." June watched Lucy. They all watched her.

She rested the paper in her lap, still seeing the words cross her mind. "That was surprising."

Kate was on the edge of her seat, and Lucy knew all the words that were about to tumble from her mouth before she said them. "This is the opportunity you have *most* desired. And I will be there. When we go up to London, we shall not be parted after all."

Grace burst into tears.

And then June pulled her close.

The youngest of the sisters sniffed. "I shall be alone. With June and Morley."

"Worse things could happen to a person," June chided, but she kissed the top of Grace's head.

Lucy watched it all happen around her as if from a cloud in the sky. So far distant, she could feel nothing. "I've wanted this very thing."

"Yes, you have, dear. Are you not pleased?" Kate reached for her hand.

"I...think I am?"

"I cannot wait to tell Logan when he arrives."

"Yes." Lucy shook her head. "Of course. I am so happy. We must respond directly." She turned to Frederick.

He nodded. "They await a response if you so desire."

"Please, bring me a parchment and ink."

The servant brought her the necessaries. Then before Lucy placed quill to page, she looked into the faces of each of her sisters. "Is this what I really truly want? To marry a duke?" Because she knew that if she went to London with the Duchess of Sussex, it would happen.

"Yes! Of course. Do you doubt it?" June searched her face. "Lucy, darling. We care not who you marry so long as you are happy. Dear Morley and Gerald have made it possible for every one of us to marry for love or at least happiness. Nothing more is required."

Lucy heard her, but she knew, deep down, that they would only be well and truly cared for if she were to secure a place in a duke's line. She knew that even her children's children would be safe if she were to do so.

She nodded. "Very well. Then yes. I shall be perfectly satisfied."

"Now that's the most romantic notion I've heard." Charity shook her head. "But at least I will gain a season in London on the heels of such romanticism. And for that, I am deter-mined to be grateful."

Lucy knew her plans for London would be well and truly different from Charity's, but she was grateful she'd been included. "And Kate. We shall dine with you at least?"

"Dine. Walk. Promenade, ball, all of the things. I shall see you every day if the duchess allows it."

"She better allow." Charity slung her arm across Lucy's shoulders. "We shall make the best of things. And we shall have each other."

"Yes." Lucy finished her acceptance of the invitation with properly grateful and pleased tones and then sent it off with the express rider.

"Goodness. This means I should begin packing. I must leave within the week." With Mr. Sullivan unharmed, and her decision to put him firmly out of her life, she should be thinking solely of her list of things to bring to London and reviewing the names of people she'd met and the associations of Lord Fellon.

And she did make a real effort to not think of Mr. Sullivan, but the tiniest memory disturbed her peace. It teased and rolled around inside, bumping against lists and propriety and all else. And only in the most pleasant of ways so she allowed it to linger. His earnest desire to hear her opinion was so astounding to her. That he considered her thoughts in order to make a choice. She might remember their conversation for a long time. And remembering was acceptable as it was likely to be the last moment of their acquaintance.

7

Days passed quickly. The duchess's carriage would arrive tomorrow. Lucy's trunks were packed. Charity's were not. Had her sister given two seconds' thought to her clothing while at her first season in London? Lucy worried she hadn't. Would the duchess be providing gowns for Charity also? Lucy hoped she would.

She exited her room to June's voice. "Charity. Take these three gowns. You must present yourself as the other ladies of the ton do so as not to garner unwanted attention."

Charity answered something with a curmudgeonly tone, and then June could be heard down the hall. "Sister. Think of Lucy. If you refuse to present yourself in a positive light for your own benefit, consider her. Don't stand in her way simply out of stubbornness. Your maid dresses you, for goodness' sake."

That was the most exasperated Lucy had heard June express in a long time. Perhaps she was starting to feel pain in her confinement.

Lucy hurried to her door. "June. You won't have the baby before we return?"

Her shocked face at Lucy's abrupt appearance turned to warmth. "Not at all. We have months yet."

"Excellent." Lucy turned to Charity. "Just bring the dresses, Charity. You'll have plenty of time to shock and amaze and other times to dress to impress."

Charity nodded.

"And I'll tell you which opportunities are which."

Charity huffed. "And why do I feel suddenly as if I'm about to be bullied about by my little sister?"

"Because you will, and you'll be happy to do so. Because I'm the reason you get to go and start up your thinking group." Lucy didn't know what to call her sister's plans precisely, but Charity had determined to collect as many people who wished to have and share thoughts on smart topics together in one location as often as possible.

June pulled both of them into a warm hug. "And I shall miss you both, dreadfully."

"And I you." Lucy kissed her sister's cheek.

When they broke away, June added, "I almost forgot. Remember we are having dinner with the Sullivans. The whole family is coming."

Lucy's breath caught in her throat. She'd not ridden her horse in days; she'd missed the rides terribly. She told herself her melancholy was not related to missing Mr. Sullivan or hearing from his own mouth the events of the other day.

"Oh, it's about time. I'm dying to hear what happened." Charity gathered the gowns June had insisted upon and made her way out the door. "I shall instruct these be included. Is everyone happy?"

"Quite." Lucy grinned, but her stomach was doing flips around inside, and she didn't know if she would have the strength to avoid this particular dinner. It was the last one at home, and then she would be off to London to be married; what harm could there be in seeing him one last time? And did she want a tray in her room for the last family dinner before she left? Certainly not. "I shall be ready for our guests."

"Oh, don't make too much of a fuss. We are trying to help them feel at ease."

"Yes."

Lucy left with plans to go over all her lists one more time and then to perhaps take a walk outside.

She was full of a new restless energy that had suddenly arisen inside, and she had to be active or she might never recover. And above all else, she must appear poised, in control, and proper for the duration of the day.

A small puff of breath escaped. In truth, for the rest of her life.

The dinner hour arrived after what seemed like an interminable afternoon waiting. She had taken extra care not to look like she took extra care. That was quite a feat, and Susan was flustered by the end of things. But Lucy felt satisfied with her appearance until she was about halfway down the stairs.

Mr. Sullivan stepped into their foyer in jacket and cravat, full dinner wear, and he looked… Her mouth went dry, and words left her mind to describe precisely how he looked. But certainly like a man who would turn many heads in a London ballroom. Thoughts of her most stunning ball gown filled her mind, ideas for a new hairstyle captured her attention, and she was in half poise to turn and flee up the stairs when June called her name. "Lucy?"

She turned back. "Yes?"

Mr. Sullivan's gaze turned to hers, and suddenly, everything around them went silent. Though she tried not to meet his gaze, to look indifferent, to focus on June, she failed at everything she tried and stared hungrily into the intense face of Mr. Sullivan. She took the remaining stairs down to join them in the entryway. With a deep curtsey, she lifted her hand to Mr. Sullivan. He bowed smartly, pressing his lips against the back of her glove. She did the same to his father. "And Mr. Sullivan." She smiled warmly. "Thank you both for coming."

The elder Mr. Sullivan chuckled. "We feel a bit as though we're putting on airs these past weeks, what with visits to the palace and now here, and dressed as gentlemen."

Mr. Sullivan the son nodded smartly. "Indeed. Who knows, Father, but these might become our most comfortable clothes."

June laughed. "Well, no matter what you wear, we are so pleased you could come. Won't you join us in the front room until the table is prepared?"

Mr. Sullivan offered his arm to June. They moved ahead which gifted Lucy a bit of space to calm her emotions and look up into young Mr. Conor Sullivan's face without anyone else looking on. "Are you well?"

"Quite well." The arm he offered was a welcome balm.

"And were not in too much danger?" Her murmurs required that he stand closer.

"Not in any, as a matter of fact."

"I'm greatly relieved to hear it."

"I would have been able to set your mind at ease, told you ten times over, had you but come to the stables." His eyes were full of questions. "Firestone feels greatly neglected."

She stepped nearer. "I thought it best."

He nodded, and his face went blank. He raised his chin and looked, as far as Lucy could see, like any other gentleman of the ton.

"No, it wasn't as if…" But she stopped. What could she say? She had been avoiding him. And she thought it for the best. It was for the best. Wasn't it? Seeing him again, especially dressed the way he was, she had to wonder what exactly was best?

They entered the room just off their dining room. And June directed the servants. "Would you please inform the others that our guests have arrived?"

The elder Mr. Sullivan did indeed look as though he would rather wear his typical stable clothing. "My daughter Margaret and Esther will be arriving in moments. They had a bit of a dress mishap, I was told, and are following shortly after."

"Those dress mishaps." June smiled and shook her head. "We are just so pleased you could come. And we are all anxious to hear the details of the heroic acts of the young Mr. Sullivan."

He dipped his head. "I'm honored to do so and to be of service." He looked to his father. "We do not take lightly the honor it has been to serve the Molyneux family and these grounds and castle."

"My son speaks truly. Our hearts are here, certainly." He shook his head.

Lucy met the son's eyes and flushed in response to the intensity she saw there.

Mr. Conor Sullivan grinned to the group. "As seen when Father denied the prince at his first request."

"What! He couldn't!" Lucy raised a hand to her mouth.

"He most certainly did."

"Well, the prince phrased things so as to give us leave to negotiate, as it were." Mr. Sullivan, Sr., cleared his throat.

"Well, we certainly must hear the whole of it."

A servant announced that the dining room was ready, and the group filed in.

June took her seat at one end of the table while everyone followed suit. When each sister surrounded the table, with Morley and Logan present also, and the food was served, June turned to the elder Mr. Sullivan. "And now, we wish to hear all the news. Has a decision been made about your work in the stables?"

Grace piped up. "And we wish to hear how it was the younger Mr. Sullivan rescued our dear Lucy." Her eyes literally glowed with gratitude. Lucy laughed. It seemed the Sullivans had more than one admirer now.

She could hardly admit such a thing, but sitting next to Mr. Conor Sullivan, walking in on his arm, she could not deny the anticipation that seemed to pulse through her.

It seemed that leaving for London was providential in more ways than one.

8

M r. Sullivan looked to his son. "You need to hear the story from my son. Though I hope he will tell the lot of it and not leave out the most exciting parts."

"Oh yes, do tell us all." Grace leaned forward.

"Well, certainly, I shall attempt to do a rather unheroic tale some justice."

"Indeed. I hardly find your efforts to rescue our Lucy unheroic." June's light censure made Mr. Sullivan smile, but it burned inside Lucy as though she'd been affronted herself. How odd to feel as though she must stand in the way of protecting Mr. Sullivan, from June, no less.

"I stand corrected. My comment was directed more at my weak participation than the worthiness of the woman being rescued. For I agree that any effort spent in protecting her or any of you would be the highest honor."

June nodded, seemingly appeased.

Lucy had not seen her thus. First losing her ease in her room upstairs and then now with the Sullivans. A part of Lucy felt a new reluctance to leave June, especially at this phase of her confinement. Lucy would return before the baby came, at least June assured her she would, but she still couldn't help but worry.

But then Mr. Conor Sullivan turned his eyes to her. "Perhaps Miss Lucy can help me remember some of the details." He cleared his throat. "We were riding back toward the castle. And we heard gunshots."

"Yes. And he commanded that I should return to the castle immediately."

"Which she did not do." He glanced apologetically at Lucy while everyone at the table gasped and called out varying types of censure.

But Lucy ignored them all. She would not have run from Mr. Sullivan while he was indeed riding into danger. "How could I when he did not? But then he tore into the woods, *toward* the guns."

Grace gasped and put hands on both sides of her face.

"But that is where my knowledge of the incident ends." Lucy turned her attention back to Mr. Conor Sullivan.

With every person at the table staring intently at him, Mr. Sullivan continued. "I admit to feeling slightly intimidated by such distinguished and beautiful attention." He turned to her but only for the briefest moments.

But that moment sent a shuddering awareness in response to him all the way through her. Did he find her beautiful? Was he speaking to her?

"I shouted back to Miss Lucy to return to the castle, and then I raced toward the sound. I knew that this lead was the closest any of us has come to actually apprehending poachers on the land. And as was seen, they are a danger."

Everyone nodded and said nothing, so he continued.

"I raced through the trees, and as I got closer, they made their first mistake."

"What was it?" Grace asked what they all wished to know.

"One of them called to the other. And then I knew two important things."

When he paused, Grace bounced in her seat. "What things?"

"I knew that they were likely in the hideout in the woods."

"There's a hideout?" Charity now seemed as excited as any of them.

"Yes, and if you would like, we can walk there after lunch."

Charity nodded. "I would most definitely wish to see it."

"Yes, I as well." Lucy nodded. "Perhaps we can go for a ride. I shall miss riding at any rate and would like another chance before I leave."

"Leave?" Mr. Sullivan's face flashed with all manner of emotion before he masked it again.

"Oh...yes."

Before she could respond, June answered for her. "She's departing for her season in London tomorrow."

He nodded.

"But what was the other thing you learned?" Charity tapped her fingers impatiently on the table.

"Oh yes." He continued, but his words sounded flat to Lucy's ears. "The other thing I knew? I knew their names."

Every lady there gasped at that revelation.

"So I confronted them."

"You know them?" Lucy knew her eyes were wide. And her concern inside grew. She couldn't really comprehend knowing a criminal.

"I do in fact. Turns out they were childhood chums of

mine. They're around town in the village as well. But as you have probably guessed, they are not a reputable family."

They sat in silence for a moment, the words hanging in the air in an uncomfortable fashion.

"When I finally reached their place of hiding, I was stunned to see a regular operation going. Pelts hanging to dry, carcasses being cut, and the latest result of their hunt being pulled out of bags. I talked with them. I challenged them. I did everything I could to keep them around, hoping help would come." He turned to Lucy with grateful eyes. "Which it did, rather sooner than I even hoped."

Lucy wanted to stare into those eyes a bit more, drinking in the gratitude, but she looked to Morley. "I happened upon the duke and Lord Morley who put things in motion immediately."

"The men resisted. But were outnumbered. And now they face prison."

Something about his expression concerned Lucy. "Do you not think imprisonment merited?"

"Oh, certainly they have broken the law. They had quite an operation going. Where I suspect they began with a few animals here and there, perhaps for dinner to feed their families, they are well beyond. In fact, if any of you were hunters, you would perhaps notice a lack in game."

Morley frowned. "But in truth, we are hunters. We just have not had a hunting party at the castle during renovations." He toyed with the food on his plate. "I hate to think of any man with family in prison, but I can't very well free him. The law is the law. And he stole from us."

"Agreed." Mr. Sullivan didn't look as though he was in complete agreement. "And certainly by now, his wife is well and cared for."

An uncomfortable feeling of guilt and responsibility hovered over the lot of them. But Charity shook her head and raised her glass. "To prison! May it be quick and instructive and help prevent further crime."

They laughed. "To prison." And everyone drank.

But Lucy wouldn't be surprised if Charity planned to bring a basket to the families of the men just in case their situation truly was dire.

The dinner continued with more typical topics being addressed. She found the Sullivans to be perfectly genteel and kind at the table, as good as they were in the stables. And though her family attempted to keep the conversation more socially inclined, soon the table talk turned to horses and purchasing and training, and the men fell deep into future plans for the growing herd of horses.

While Lucy listened, she couldn't find any indication as to whether they were moving to the prince's stables or not. And for some reason, she wished for them to stay. Was that fair to Mr. Sullivan? Would it not be a better situation for them were they to have the stamp of approval from the royal family? She didn't know much about any of it, but she didn't want to lose the Sullivans. And truth be told, they belonged at the castle. They'd been there before any of the sisters had arrived. But most of all, her thoughts were selfishly directed. She'd come to expect the steady and friendly hand of Mr. Sullivan to assist her with her horses and, of late, to ride at her side. And she knew she wasn't prepared for that to end.

Silly talk, she knew it to be, but the thoughts continued anyway. If things moved forward as expected, she would be marrying Lord Fellon and would be using his stables.

She cleared her throat, curiosity burning enough that she spoke. "You said you denied the prince the first time."

Both Mr. Sullivans turned to her, the expression on the younger still carefully guarded.

"Yes, we did, miss." Mr. Sullivan's older kindly eyes were a comfort to her, the kind of eyes that made you wish for a warm fire and a place with a good book.

"I think she's wondering about another request from the prince?" The young Mr. Sullivan tipped his head to her.

"Conor, I do believe you are correct."

Conor. Lucy smiled. *Conor Sullivan.* The name rolled around on her tongue. Hearing it spoken out loud had been intriguing, sounded Irish. Her mind went to the tapestry. O'Sullivan. But the Sullivans were still talking. She tried to pay attention even though her mind was skipping with possibilities.

"When the prince asked the second time, Father again refused him."

Everyone at the table gasped.

"He had improved his offer. But it was not what Conor here wanted." Mr. Sullivan's look of pride in his son was obvious and large. "But then His Highness came back with the sweetest of deals. And we are both grateful. Will be to our dying day." Then old Mr. Sullivan got choked up, and Lucy looked from one Sullivan to the other.

June leaned forward. "What was this most magnanimous offer?"

The father looked to the son, as words seemed to have left him.

"What Father would tell you, I'm certain, is that he is most grateful and recognizes that this is the chance of a lifetime for the Sullivan family, one that we have been awaiting for generations."

Lucy thought his words peculiar and intriguing, and suddenly, a thousand questions raced through her mind. "The prince understands our desire to make something of ourselves, our own standing business. To enter in trade and to be landholders one day." Conor Sullivan's eyes flicked to gaze at her, but only for a second. In that second, the truth of his words made an impression on her soul. Something happened deep inside that she knew wouldn't be leaving any time soon. Mr. Sullivan wished to be a landholder. She nodded to herself, unaware of any other sound in the room.

Then she refocused.

"He has said that we can work for him and oversee the horses here at the castle, we can hire more staff to do so if needed, that he has staff at the castle but he would like Father and myself to be the headmasters. And…"

Everyone at the table leaned in.

"And he will help us establish ourselves. He will offer the crown approval and will recommend us. As long as we give five years to his personal stables and get them up and running under someone who we personally train." He adjusted his shoulders.

Then the elder Mr. Sullivan spoke again. "The prince hoped that Conor here would be the one to take over for a time, but he is the most ambitious of the two of us. Seems he wants to regain the Sullivan name."

And here it was again, that idea that something intriguing was amiss in their family line.

"Regain?" June had forgotten all about the uneaten food on her plate, apparently. They all had.

The young Mr. Sullivan cut back in. "Father tells the story of an original branch from Ireland, attached to this castle somehow. There are stories that there's a connection there, but the specifics are lost. There was a falling-out or some kind of family scandal, and we aren't certain."

"Except for our family crest. And the heirlooms."

"Crest? Heirlooms?" Lucy's mouth went dry. What was happening here in this conversation? Who were the Sullivans?

"Do you believe you are related somehow to the families who lived here?"

Mr. Sullivan snorted. "Highly unlikely. Why would we be running the stables if we were related to the royals who lived here?" He dipped his head. "Beggin' your pardon if I sound coarse. And nothing but respect for the families who are associated with the castle."

"We are associated with the castle." Lucy cleared her throat. Her words were coming out breathy and way more excitable sounding than she would ever wish to portray. "We have recently learned how much of our direct line of relations are all tied to this castle."

"How have you learned such a thing?" Mr. Sullivan's eyes were now more interested than she'd ever seen them.

The sisters all exchanged glances.

Then Morley called for the servants to bring in the tapestry. "We can lay it out in the morning room where we have more light."

As he stood, June shook her head. "But we haven't finished eating." Morley would have returned to his seat, but then she shook her head again. "This is too exciting for food. If we must, we can ask for food to be warmed for us."

Everyone seemed to be in agreement.

Lucy left the room on Mr. Sullivan's arm, and he was strangely quiet. But there seemed to be so much to say. "These are some amazing developments."

He nodded.

"What will you do?"

"I suppose I'll be a very busy stable hand for another five years." Something in his tone did not sound as cheerful as she would have hoped.

"Is that not the most excellent news of your life?" She pressed her fingers into his arm. Surely, he could see that he had much to celebrate. "You can do anything, be anything, rise as you said you wished."

"That is all true, almost." He turned to her, and there was an uncertainty, a pain in his eyes that she did not understand.

But before she could press further, they were in the morning room and the servants were unrolling the tapestry.

"Do you know the names of your ancestors that would have had the closest relationship?" Morley stood next to the elder Mr. Sullivan who was hungrily searching the tapestry already.

"If you see here," June pointed to the Molyneaux name at the top of the tree, "we are putting things together to determine just how and who is related through this line. That right there is our great-grandfather." She pointed to where the line stopped.

"And that is ours." Mr. Sullivan pointed to the last O'Sullivan on the line, before the empty space where everything seemed to cut off. "Our great-great-, rather."

They stared in silence for several moments, Lucy for one trying to piece together what that could possibly mean.

"But what happened?" Lucy turned to Conor Sullivan.

"We don't know. This is one of Father's tales—"

"It is most definitely a true tale, if it must be a tale. We have the crest. The armory, the signet ring."

"Father." Conor Sullivan's teeth ground around inside a suddenly tight jaw.

"There is nothing to be afraid of here, son. This secret has been kept long enough."

"And I say it can die a secret. We are making our own name for ourselves. The Sullivans. We don't need to prove anything."

"Not a proof, but I'm proud of who we are."

"I as well." Conor Sullivan glanced quickly around the table. "Forgive us. We can have our age-old family discussion in private."

"But we would like to know. We have had our own discussions about this line and what has transpired. You see?" June pointed to it. "If you are the O'Sullivans, then our great-great-grandfathers might have been cousins."

"Which would make you of noble, if not royal, blood." Lucy wanted to shake him for his reluctance. This was news indeed and of the best kind.

"And is that all that matters? What about honor? And relations to people who you can be proud of? What of hard work, and making your own honest living, what of this branch of the Sullivans; the two standing right here? Father, we are the Sullivans." He spoke with more passion than she had ever seen in a man. Everyone she knew was so contained, so restrained, so...bored. But the energy and emotion that lit his face and enlivened his words were alluring. She stood at his side but wanted to be even closer. His strength filled her with the same. She wanted to drink it in, to feel that passion rise up inside. She'd never felt anything quite like what he was demonstrating. Or at least, she'd never let it outside of her. There was that energy deep inside that no one ever saw, that desire for freedom. It came out when she rode. His words tapped into that. And suddenly she wanted to be out in the wind on the cliffs more than she ever had before. She craved the cool wind and the open sky and all of a sudden wished to stand with arms out at her side and spin in a circle.

She knew her cheeks must be flushed.

Charity glanced in her direction more than once.

Lucy realized that everyone in the room who was staring at Conor Sullivan's outburst would now be looking at her as well. But there was nothing for it but to stand still and hope she wasn't a spectacle.

After a long moment between father and son, Conor Sullivan dipped his head. "Forgive me. Again, these conversations are certainly best had at home." He glanced around at everyone in the room but Lucy. "Forgive me."

"There is nothing to forgive, certainly." Morley clapped the elder Mr. Sullivan on the back. "You say you have evidence of the relation? Perhaps further information to the story?"

Conor stiffened beside her, but Lucy was grateful he held his tongue.

"We do. Would you like to come and see?"

"Yes, we would." June nodded. "This is grand news indeed and so fitting that you've had such a boon of opportunity, is it not?"

"Yes, I believe so." Mr. Sullivan glanced at his son but then looked away. "Grand news indeed."

Just at that moment, the Sullivan daughter and mother showed up at the front door.

Conor Sullivan groaned quietly. What was his concern? That they were so late, showing poor manners, or that more of his family would be talking about the tapestry, or what?

But then the two entered, and she felt she could guess.

"Oh, there you are!" Mrs. Sullivan all but shrieked as she

moved forward with hands out. "I've brought pie." She waved her daughter forward.

The footman belatedly announced, "A Mrs. Esther Sullivan and a Miss Margaret Sullivan."

They curtseyed at this point, if you could call their downward motions almost stumbling on their own feet a curtsey.

Conor stood so stiffly at her side she wasn't certain that he could bend at all, anywhere.

"And here's the missus." Mr. Sullivan nodded toward his wife.

"We do apologize for being late. We could not get Margaret in her stays." Mrs. Sullivan giggled. "They certainly are more difficult for the greater endowed of us, aren't they?" She turned to Jane and then to the others, probably realizing that not one of them was particularly well endowed in the manner in which she described. And none of them wished to discuss such things either. Lucy was amazed, and where moments before her new interest in Conor Sullivan seemed founded on possibly a genuinely sound bloodline, she now realized how plagued with unpredictability his family would undoubtedly be. Nothing like the staid and practiced manners of the ton, this family could do anything at any moment, enter a home with an obvious lack of manners or any other similar thing. Would she be having dinner parties and ask the Sullivan family not to attend?

A whole life ahead of the repercussions of being married to a servant flashed before her eyes, and though she would never have pegged herself as a snob, she realized that there were definite reasons that the noble classes married only within their own stations.

And with that realization, a great sigh escaped.

Which caused the jerk of Conor's head and a new hurt in his eyes.

Lucy shook her head. "No." Her voice was low.

But Conor stepped away. "Thank you, Mother, sister, for the pies, perhaps we can just leave them as we were on our way out the door?"

"Quite right." Morley stepped in that direction as well. "I want to see if we can unravel more of the mystery. We all do, don't we?"

"Most certainly." June rested a hand on his arm.

And so it was that the entire group made their way to the Sullivan home.

9

L ucy rode with her sisters. The men took the other carriage, and some of the Sullivans rode in the cart they had come in.

And nothing in Lucy's orderly world made sense.

She wished to hide in her room.

Only the most ardent feelings of curiosity kept her from crying off with a headache.

They pulled up in front of the Sullivan home. Every other time she'd been to the place, she had been charmed. Every other time she'd spoken with Mrs. Sullivan, she'd felt the warmth of her motherly goodness. Why during this meeting did everything seem off? Why was she comparing and expecting more from them than was their station?

Was she so shallow?

No, she was not. She was practical.

And that's how she'd always been. And that's how it was going to be. She stepped down from her carriage, determined to be as she always had been, to love this family as they deserved to be loved, as fellow human beings, to see Mr.

Conor Sullivan as a good stable hand with a great opportunity ahead, to be grateful for all that life had given her, and to leave tomorrow for London so that she could marry Lord Fellon and become a duchess.

The thoughts stole her breath for a moment. And for the first time, a wave of insecurity crashed through her sensibility. A duchess? What did she know about being a duchess?

Her hands shook as she clasped them together to hide her emotion. With chin high and feet purposely steady in her walk, she made her way to the front door with the others.

"Please forgive the state of the place." Mrs. Sullivan paused. "In fact, will you give me a moment?" She winked and stepped inside, giving no one a view of the interior as she closed the door swiftly behind her.

June laughed. "I can well imagine."

Margaret nodded. "It's the stays. I think she's cleaning up the extra dresses too."

Stays had already been mentioned way too many times for Lucy's liking.

The men approached.

Mr. Sullivan called out, "Go on in. We've got nothing to hide in there."

Lucy opened her mouth to protest, but then Mrs. Sullivan opened the door herself. Her face was flushed and a few dots of perspiration lined her brow, but she smiled in her habitually warm manner. "Please come in."

"Thank you."

"Can I get you anything?"

"Oh no, don't trouble yourself as we are still technically in the act of offering dinner." June shook her head. "You must all return for dessert at the very least."

"We are honored by your hospitality." Mrs. Sullivan's

curtsey at this point was proper and beautifully done. She was as proper as Lucy had ever seen her. Perhaps the earlier scene was simply a figment of Lucy's over anticipatory mind. Perhaps created by dashed hopes that the Sullivans were in fact noble.

Another thought plagued her. No matter what that tapestry tree said, the Sullivans were a product of their upbringing.

Was that not the same for the Standish sisters?

Her breathing picked up, and her heart tried to keep pace. She wrung her hands.

And then Charity was at her side. "Are you well, sister?"

Lucy shook her head.

"Perhaps a moment?" She tugged her toward the front door.

"Yes, thank you."

June called after them, but Charity waved her off. "We'll just be a moment."

When the front door was closed, Charity walked with her a safe from hearing distance and then murmured, "What is going on?"

"I don't know." Her voice shook. "What if we're frauds? What if we're noble in name only just like them and that everyone around us can see the evidence in our abhorrent manners?"

"What are you talking about? I thought for sure you were going to tell me you were besotted with Conor Sullivan." She shook her head. "But this is all about your appearance of properness?"

Charity's tone left much to be desired in Lucy's opinion. And it rankled so much that her ire was risen in such a way that she had the strength to push aside her insecurities. "I refuse to be baited into this conversation. The fact of the matter is I could no sooner be besotted with Conor Sullivan as I could with our footman James." There. She said it. And while she was still struggling to believe her own words, she could move forward with the strength of her pride, with her reactions to Charity's digs.

But Conor Sullivan closed the front door behind him and, without a glance in their direction, hurried toward the stables.

She sucked in a most desperate breath, for she felt as though her lungs had all but frozen. "Did he hear?"

"I don't know."

"Are we not far enough away?"

"I think we are."

Lucy let her head fall. "Perhaps I should just go back to the castle. Will you please tell me what you all learn?"

"Yes, certainly. Ask one of the coachmen or a footman to attend."

She nodded, only half hearing as her steps moved toward the castle.

Lucy found a letter on her nightstand when she entered the room. Susan peeked her head around the corner and then joined her with a curtsey. "The mail came while you were out. Will you be wanting to prepare for bed?"

"Yes, please. Give me a moment first."

"Yes, miss."

She sat with her letter. It looked to be from Gerald and Amelia. The duke had gone home just yesterday. Could this have come by express? But when she broke the seal, she recognized Amelia's hand.

With a soft breath of hope, she settled into what she hoped were lovely words to distract her.

My dear Lucy,

I hear you are to be joining us in London, or rather you

shall be at the duchess's beck and call in London. She is the most adept woman to have on your side as you prepare for a season, that I know. With your goals, you are in good hands.

Gerald mentioned to me, of course, that you and he discussed a particular situation there, one of feelings. I will not bring it up again if you don't wish to discuss it or if the purpose no longer applies, but I for one must counsel you to act with your best interests in mind. Only follow after such a course if the most desperate and ardent feelings dictate your actions. As the child of a family divided, it does not come without its challenges, made simpler by the name and power of a dukedom.

These were not the comforting words or the balm of distraction Lucy had hoped she would receive.

The rest of the letter talked of having her to dinner, of visits to the museums, and of good books she must read from Amelia's library.

And by the end, Lucy was well and truly looking forward to London.

Conor Sullivan and the entire Sullivan family, no matter who they were related to, were firmly out of her mind.

Almost.

She was prepared for bed, her candles extinguished, by the time the noise of the others returning alerted her. But she stayed firmly in place. By sheer force of will, she resisted every inclination to step into the hall and hear the whole of their evening.

But sleep alluded her.

And after many hours, she threw off the covers, grabbed a robe and some slippers, and stepped out into the hall.

Everything was quiet.

And all was dark.

The soft padding of her feet was almost audible in the silence of the house.

She stepped down the stairs. Still seeing no one, she moved to the back servants' entrance and stepped outside into the night air.

Where she was going, she had only the tiniest inkling, but she knew she must go. And when she arrived in front of Firestone, it was as if destiny itself brought her there.

"There, girl."

Firestone poked her nose out over the gate and nuzzled her.

"You gonna miss me?" She leaned her head against the diamond of white. "I know I'm gonna miss you."

They stood like that. The horse was quiet and still in a moment of understanding.

"At least you're fit for the duke's household. And even if you weren't, you're with me."

Fit for the duke's household.

A measure she'd created to work against, to push herself, to challenge and attain all these years, with the hopes that she, with her marriage, could solidify their place in the nobility to ensure that no Standish woman would ever be without again, nor their children, or children's children.

She considered her own family tree. She'd come from nobility, from William the Conqueror himself. And yet, the man's brother's children's children's children and on and on were suffering in this generation, or they had been until Gerald stepped in.

Her next puff of air made Firestone antsy. She jerked her head back.

"Sorry, girl."

There really wasn't a way to ensure stability and security

forever. She shrugged. But marrying into a dukedom was her best possible chance.

Movement startled her, from the shadows in the corner.

"Who's there?"

Conor Sullivan stepped forward.

"Oh!" She brought a hand up to her neckline, closing it tighter around her neck, though she was well and truly more covered in her robe than she would be in a ball gown.

"I wondered if you would come."

"Have you been waiting?"

He stepped closer, into the moonlight from a window. Something about him in the half dark, the light on his hair, his face half hidden, made him even more handsome or perhaps made it easier to pretend again that he was well mannered and noble. He was well mannered, she reminded herself.

"Did they tell you?"

She shook her head. "I was in bed."

"But you couldn't sleep."

"No."

"Do you want to know?"

"Does it matter?"

He eyed her for a moment with pressed lips and then with a drop of his shoulders shook his head. "I don't think it does." He sat in a heap on the bench below the window. And he looked so dejected that she moved immediately to sit beside him.

10

Lucy sat close enough that she felt the warmth from Conor Sullivan's body, but they did not touch. His eyes were closed, his shoulders slumped, his head leaning back against the wall behind him.

"Were you waiting here for me?"

He nodded.

"Do you wish to tell me? Even if it doesn't matter?" Had she totally deflated his purpose in wishing to talk with her? Surely, she could listen.

"No, I do not wish to tell you." He lifted his head and turned dark eyes to her. With the moonlight behind his face, he looked more mysterious than ever. "But I shall, because you will hear it from the others by and by, and Father seems bound and determined to make known our sordid past."

"Sordid?"

"Our O'Sullivan ancestor was the son of a noble and commoner union that so displeased the remaining branches of the family that we were cut off, our heritage erased and knowledge of us hidden to future generations. The couple were shunned and kept hidden who they really were, preferring life as commoners than the hissing and cutting from their noble relations." His use of the word "noble" held a bit of a sneer to it, and Lucy could well see the irony of those with the worst manners being those who had been trained and should know better.

"And so they changed from O'Sullivan to Sullivan?" She tilted her head. "Doesn't sound very different."

"No, it doesn't, and they didn't go far, did they?" He shrugged. "I do believe they tried to find work elsewhere, but there was an O'Sullivan who valued their knowledge of horses and paid them handsomely to stay."

She nodded. "And here you are."

"And here I am."

She felt like she should say something to help him see the benefit of his situation because he truly didn't have much to complain about in that moment. "Like you said to all of us, you are making your own Sullivan name, you are working toward something special and will one day be a landholder." She smiled, and though she was suddenly overly tired, she tried to look and sound as encouraging as possible.

"But it won't be soon enough, will it?"

Soon enough. She held her breath. Was he talking about her? Soon enough for them? She shook her head, trying to find the words, any word.

"Say nothing. Your face says it all." He stood with his back to her. "You leave tomorrow?"

"Yes." Her voice sounded quiet even to her ears, but somehow, she knew he heard.

"Then Godspeed." He didn't face her again but walked in the direction of the door.

"That's it?"

He paused. Then his shoulders dropped again, and he turned. "That's it." His face was once again fully hidden in the shadows. She had no idea what he was thinking and daren't say much more, because he was right. That was it.

He stepped to the door just as a large man came barreling in. "Lucy!"

She stood up and squealed. "Morley!"

He pushed into Conor's chest, backing him up against the wall. Though Conor was large, as large as Morley, he did not resist. But he held his hands up. "This is not what you think."

While pinning Conor in place, Morley turned to Lucy. "Are you well?"

She nodded and moved toward him. "Yes. I came to say goodbye to Firestone. Conor." She gasped. "I mean, Mr. Sullivan." She wished to dig her own place of hiding at the most unfortunate slip of using his first name. "Mr. Sullivan was here as well, and we talked. I asked him the story of his family because I missed it earlier."

"And you told him you are traveling to London tomorrow with hopes to marry Lord Fellon?"

"Yes, that was mentioned."

Morley stared a moment more into Conor's face and then backed away. "Thank you, sir, for being a gentleman."

He stood taller. "I am but a stable hand, but in the regard you refer, I have always behaved in a manner most proper."

"Yes, and we thank you for that. Your manners and your honor are impeccable. Forgive my brash assumptions."

Conor nodded, looked one more time at Lucy, and then walked out the door.

Lucy fell back to the bench. "Woosh!"

Then Morley came to sit beside her. "Are you well, truly?"

And with that one question, she could no longer speak, her lips quivered, and her shoulders tightened up as sobs burst out of her.

He pulled her up against his chest. "There."

"I don't know what's wrong with me."

"Nor I, but June has taught me that sometimes there doesn't even have to be a definable thing wrong." He patted her head.

And Lucy laughed. "That is perhaps the truest thing you have ever said." She sniffed. "But at that brief outburst, I feel somewhat better." She studied him. "Why are you out at this hour?"

"June. She went to find you in your room and, when you weren't there, sent me here."

A feeling of trepidation tugged at her. "Are they all awake then?"

"Yes, I'm afraid you've caused quite a stir."

"Oh dear."

"Shall I keep the matter of the young Mr. Sullivan between us?"

"If you could, yes. Please."

"Consider it forgotten."

"Thank you."

He held out his arm which Lucy gratefully took, and then he led her out of the barn and back up toward the house.

Faces in the window peered out at them, and then the unmistakable hand of Grace waved. Then she ran from the window, and another face appeared.

"Yes, there they are." She smiled. "I am grateful to be so loved."

"As you should be." He tilted toward her. "You will be

missed while in London. But June tells me you are planning to return for the birth of our new son?"

"Or daughter, yes. I wouldn't miss it and will crave any and all reports on the matter of her confinement."

"We will keep you and all apprised, certainly." He stared straight ahead. Even in the dark lighting, Lucy could see tired lines on his face.

"You've done wonderful things for us, Morley, thank you."

"You are most welcome. I've loved you ladies as family from the beginning."

"A more benevolent caretaker we could have never asked for, nor a more loving brother."

"And that I shall ever be. Even when we must move to my own family seat."

"Yes, even then." She sighed. "Though I don't know how Grace will take it."

"Well, one of you needs to live here. This must be the seat of someone. Don't you think?"

Lucy was struck for a moment of shock. "You know? I never thought of that. If we all marry men with estates, no one will care first for the castle." She shook her head at the thought. "Perhaps Charity." She laughed. "But surely, she will marry as well, won't she?"

Morley joined her in laughter. "I couldn't say, but there are certainly enough men willing to give it a go."

"We shall definitely have a time of it."

"And may I wish you the very best if I don't get a word in edgewise as soon as we walk through that door?"

"You may, and thank you."

"You are welcome."

The servants' entrance burst open, and June, Charity, and Grace flowed out into the night with outstretched arms.

"We have been worried about you, sister." Grace kissed her cheek.

"Thank you, Morley." June stepped up to Lucy's other side. Charity studied her. "And here I thought she'd be blushing in embarrassment at a romantic interlude."

Lucy gasped. "Charity, really."

"I know, I know, hopes dashed. You're far too practical for that."

Lucy didn't want to talk about it. The meeting with Conor Sullivan was unsettling enough, the implications of being caught thus condemning enough without the thought of anything truly scandalous happening between them.

"Firestone and I have a relationship enough." She smiled. Then sighed. "I'm going to miss that horse." She squeezed her sisters extra tight. "And the lot of you. Somehow, I don't think the duchess's home will be quite so liberal with the hugs and late-night talks."

"Not unless you consider late-night balls. You, sister, are going to have festivity enough for any person, I'd imagine."

"And I shall find ways to fill your days as well as your nights." Charity grinned. "We shall take the town by storm, and Kate when she can join us."

Lucy wondered about that. Just what did Charity have up her sleeves? Nothing too improper, Lucy hoped. Nothing too bluestocking, she prayed.

"Oh, stop your concerns, I'm well aware of your sensibilities."

"Thank you, sister. I'm certain we shall find enough between the two of us to fill any sane person's calendar."

"Let us hope."

They made their way up the stairs together, and at her door, Lucy turned. "I do apologize for causing anyone worry. That was most inconsiderate and most unwise, I realize."

"Yes, please, you know not to do such things in London…" June's concern brought more remorse.

"Oh, sister. I do. I will not be so foolhardy in London. I promise."

She studied her face a moment and then nodded. "Good night then."

This time when Lucy rested her head on the pillow, she fell asleep almost before she could think two thoughts; at least, those were all the things she remembered upon waking in the morning. The look of Conor Sullivan's face right before he walked out the door, and the feeling she had when he'd told her that he was indeed of noble birth. Neither bore a repeat in her mind, for thoughts of Conor Sullivan as anything other than her stable hand were as unproductive as any.

11

With the trunks on the roof and she and Charity snuggled inside the carriage, maids in tow and surrounded by footmen and coachmen, they couldn't be any more secure. Lucy smiled at the outpouring of love and care all the while Charity huffed. "It's as if we haven't been to London before."

"To be fair, the last time we went, we were very young."

"True." She waved and smiled until they were down the drive and out of sight. Then she pulled out her journal. "Now, to review my plans." Her face looked too excited, her eyes gleamed a bit too much.

"Charity?"

She didn't answer at first and turned a page.

"Sister."

When her lashes lifted and she met Lucy's gaze, she responded with an overly innocent expression. "And what has you all ruffled?"

"What are you scheming, sister?"

"I'm always scheming. Why should today be any different?"

"Because you are scheming a particularly large amount right now. What exactly are your plans for your time in London?" She'd been so consumed with her own distractions she hadn't given Charity much thought, and the longer she watched her devour the written plans for their stay, the more concerned she became.

"I am scheming a normal amount. But, Lucy, I've never been in London as an adult. All the big thinkers will be there. Everyone I read about, every author, the women who make a difference, the bluestockings." She said that last bit with a worshipful gaze, and it was then that Lucy knew she needed to perhaps set some ground rules. "Before you know it, I'll have us accepted in all the most respected reading salons, the soirees, the luncheons. We will be dining and talking with the greats of our day if I have anything to say about it. Imagine—"

"I must interrupt the raptures."

Charity closed her mouth. "What is it?"

"These parties, these groups, bluestockings and the like… they aren't really my goal for the trip."

Charity considered her. "I'm assuming you mean that these kinds of people would not be welcome at the parties where you hope to be invited."

"I don't know precisely where they would be welcome, but I really have only one goal for this trip."

Charity nodded. "Understood." Though her face looked pinched for a moment, she seemed to rally, for which Lucy was relieved. "I would never want to hurt your chances with Lord Fellon."

"Thank you. Because you know I support you. I do. I

believe in thinking women, in good education. I am fascinated with all manner…" Lucy stopped, because from what she could gather, Charity was already deep into her written plans and no longer heard what Lucy said.

When she didn't notice Lucy's pause in conversation, Lucy felt justified in pulling out her own book and reading instead of trying to pacify Charity.

But she could not feel distracted enough with just the words to entertain her. The moment the carriage quieted, Conor Sullivan's gruff farewell returned to her mind. If he hadn't been so gruff, if they'd left on more congenial terms, she'd likely feel comfortable with things. But as they were, she found it hard to ignore the unfinished sense of missing peace that lingered with thoughts of him. And that disquiet was niggling at her.

With a sigh, she tossed her book on the seat beside her.

No one noticed. Both maids were either sleeping or feigning sleep, and Charity was as engrossed as ever in her thoughts. Lucy would not be surprised if she pulled out an inkwell and began writing right there in the carriage.

And so Lucy did the only thing she could think of to entertain her restless mind and shut the door on further thoughts of Conor Sullivan. She thought about Lord Fellon.

He enjoyed a good promenade in the park. And he usually went right before lunch. But most of the ladies of the ton knew that, and so they too would walk during that hour and were often seen surrounding him. Lucy had learned that he also liked to go in the cool of the evening when fewer people were out. During those hours, he was more introspective, and in truth, Lucy liked him best on their twilight-hour walks. In Brighton. Hopefully, his habits were similar in London.

He was quite good at fencing and would talk at great

length about his latest win if asked. He was impassioned about horses but still did not know Lucy also held an interest in them. He was mostly kind to others but often made fun of the bluestockings among them. Which Lucy was all too keenly aware would happen as soon as he learned of Charity and her new friends. He dressed smartly. He appreciated when Lucy wore blue. He loved to dance the reels and was tolerable at the waltz. Pity since Lucy loved the waltz. But all things could be learned.

For conversation, he mostly stuck to the conventions. Weather, gossip, and his latest book. Which was another item in his favor. The man loved to read. Lucy could scarcely keep up with him. But she made a real effort, and when he would mention a book, she rushed off to find a copy and read it.

He was tall, handsome, well-mannered, and, most important of all, would be a duke someday. What more could she want in a man?

And would he ask her to marry him? All indications said that he would. But time would tell; she couldn't waste a moment, nor did she have room for mistakes.

She reviewed her own personal rules of deportment. Do not speak loudly. Do not giggle. Do not talk of herself. Ask the right questions. Sit still. Be graceful. Be gracious. Include others. Do not smile overly large. Do not slouch. She stopped. That list was depressing, and she had it memorized.

What more could she do that would ease the decision for Lord Fellon?

As ideas began to formulate, she knew that in actuality she would need to rely on the Duchess of Sussex and her relationship with Lord Fellon's mother, the Duchess of Stratton.

"That's it!" Lucy's voice carried across the carriage. Both

maids jumped from sleep, and Charity lifted her chin to study her.

"I do apologize, but I've had a splendid idea."

Everyone returned to their previous activities. Lucy would take tea with the duchess. She would renew her efforts by spending more time with the mother. None of which sounded life altering, but Lucy realized how remiss she had been in this area in the past. But with the Duchess of Sussex at her side, all those doors would be open and plenty more besides. She would need to remember to thank the woman. What a provident offer. With all of the ton opened up to Lucy, she would surely make a fine match of it, one that would aid their family for decades, if not forever.

And perhaps—another idea tickled her brain. She tapped her chin. Perhaps it would help the duke if there were some competition for her hand. The last time he was in Brighton, there were a few lords who circled around her, and Lord Fellon seemed to try harder when he was having to beat someone else out for the attention.

She made a mental list of all the eligible men of her acquaintance that might serve this very purpose until the names swam before her eyes. She bored herself with her plans, so much so that her eyes closed, at last succumbing to the swift passage of time that sleep offered, and she awoke only when they were about to arrive.

"The duchess does have a lovely estate." Charity opened the window, and a crisp, fresh air circulated in and around them, exhilarating Lucy's mind. As she stretched her arms above her head, she peered out.

The grounds were lovely and orderly. She liked that. It was one of few homes with enviable grounds in London. Though they sat a small distance from the park, they boasted a beautiful hedgerow, rose gardens, and even a bit of a walking path from the looks of things. The carriage pulled in front of the large pillared entrance. Servants piled out of the house, and the duchess herself descended.

"My, to what do we owe this grand welcome!" Charity raised an eyebrow and then straightened her skirts as a footman opened their door. "You best descend first." Charity held an arm out toward the door.

Lucy lifted her chin and reached for the footman's hand. As she stepped down out of the carriage and onto the rocky drive, she prepared herself for this new life. And then her eyes turned to her new mentor.

The Duchess of Sussex stood tall, and her eyes danced with approval. "So you have arrived." She held out her hands as Lucy curtseyed low. "Come, child. Let's have a good look at you."

She spun Lucy about, this way and that, and said "hmm" plenty of times before she nodded. "This shall be quite the adventure for you and I. I daresay not a man in the ton will be able to resist you when we're through."

A new wariness arose inside. "Surely we don't need every man in the ton…"

"Oh tosh, it's just talk. But certainly if the most sought-after men are interested, then it goes to follow that every other man would be as well." She turned to walk Lucy into the house, her hands on the crook of Lucy's arm.

But being a sister as well as an opportunist, she turned. "Charity was so pleased to be invited."

The duchess paused as well. "Ah yes, the sister. You, my dear, will instruct me on all the ways of the more crude and educated crowd. I wish to hear of the bluestocking ways and their undertakings."

Charity curtseyed. "I shall be pleased to engage in all manner of conversations."

"I'm certain you shall." She waved. "Come, let us all convene in the front room where a small repast has been provided. Then you shall wash up and prepare yourselves for the modiste." She smiled, obviously pleased with herself. "I've even told them to measure you for a dress, Charity. This shall be great fun. We three will have all the delights."

Lucy warmed further toward her. "I don't know how to begin to thank you. With you as my guide, I know I shall succeed."

"You don't need to go thanking me anymore. Once was sufficient." She patted her hand. "But I'm pleased as can be, make no mistake. I told you once that you would be the Standish daughter to marry a duke, did I not say such a thing?"

"You did."

"And we all remember." Charity's tone was deceptively bland. And Lucy wondered just what was going on in her head.

But they continued into the front room where a table was spread with all manner of delicious things. Meats, fruits, cheeses, spreads, bread, cakes. Lucy's stomach rumbled.

"Ah. Hungry, are you? Please let us indulge. It takes a healthy and well-fed constitution to weather the visit we will have. This modiste is the best in London, with a healthy understanding of French fashion and an impeccable taste in fabrics. She is precise, and we will be together for hours."

Lucy couldn't hide her smile. "I will attempt to remember you do not wish for a constant stream of gratitude, but I must thank you once more, this sounds too good for words. I shall love every moment, I'm certain."

"Yes, you probably shall." The duchess's smile was

kindly, warm. And Lucy was relieved she did not seem at all condescending or overly proud of her charitable assistance. Instead, she was more like an elderly relation. Some of the anxious tightness in her chest loosened at that thought. Perhaps the season would be more enjoyable than she planned.

Just as they'd both had their fill and were headed up the stairs, the butler announced, "The Duchess of York to see you."

"Oh, what does she want?" The Duchess of Sussex's grumblings made Lucy laugh. She covered her lips with her fingers, but when she and Charity shared a glance, she couldn't help the laugh that bubbled up. How familiar and yet foreign this all sounded. How many years had these two duchesses competed for charitable excess on behalf of the Standish sisters? How often had they come with last year's cast-off gowns? How many times had they both expounded on the virtue of provident living and mourned with the family their plight? And now here they were, gloating that their prized choice charity had risen above itself.

When Charity and Lucy rose from their welcoming curt-seys to the newly arrived duchess, she looked them over before holding out her hands. "Come to me, girls. This is a day I'm certain none of us thought we would ever see."

They approached and kissed the duchess.

She reached a hand out to Lucy's face. "There's a girl now. Yes, you will certainly make something of yourself. If you find a need for more elevated company, please come to tea, we can make our own plans..." The side glance she gifted the Duchess of Sussex with those remarks brought a snort out of Charity.

The Duchess of York turned discerning eyes in Charity's

direction. "Oh, and you're here as well, are you? Have you come to astound the ton with your new theories on polite society?" Her eyebrow rose but only in a playful tease. It appeared that perhaps she supported Charity and her different approach? Lucy's hope rose.

"It is wonderful to see you again, Your Grace."

As they all returned to their seats and the Duchess of York sipped her tea, Lucy prepared herself to start answering questions about Lord Fellon and her plans while in London. She almost choked on her tea when the Duchess of York leaned forward and said, "So, Charity, when is our first meeting of the bluestockings?"

Without missing a beat, Charity replaced her teacup, brushed an errant hair from her face, and grinned. "As soon as you'd like me to plan one."

Lucy listened to the women plan how the Duchess of York could ease herself into a meeting or two with these more radical-thinking women. In some ways, she was grateful for the time away from the spotlight, after a long carriage ride and with much to think about herself.

But the conversation continued through another tray of tea, and at that point, Lucy was tired. So tired that when the butler announced the modiste, she jumped to her feet. "Excellent!"

Though her eyebrows raised in slight disapproval at Lucy's sudden leap to her feet, the Duchess of York waved Lucy on with the Duchess of Sussex at her side.

The modiste was led into a different room, a similarly appointed parlor. Servants followed with bolts of fabric, ribbons, and books. Lucy had had ball gowns made, of course, and the modiste in Brighton was one of the best, recommended by Kate herself who was knowledgeable and picky about these things. But Lucy had never seen the likes of this woman.

With a delightful French accent, she began to work on Lucy's wardrobe for the season, and the longer she planned, the more relieved Lucy felt. She would present the correct image, the proper manners, and a congenial nature. Surely, she would be a success. Or the best-dressed spectacular failure, she admitted with a small inner laugh.

But she hummed to herself while the two older women discussed color. And she told herself she was satisfied.

Hours later, with Charity at her side walking the grounds of their temporary London residence, Lucy allowed herself to unwind. "I don't think I shall move an inch when I fall into bed tonight."

"Nor I, though I have some writing and some correspondence. The duchess would be a huge boon to our meetings. Her connections, her resources." Charity reached out to break a leaf off the hedge at their side. "I would have never guessed, all these years of knowing that woman, that she had a radical movement tendency."

"Well, I don't know. Perhaps we've underestimated her. What kind of woman goes out of their way to visit five destitute sisters?"

"The kind who would also work for change. You are so correct, sister. She's a gold mine. And I shall forever be grateful to you and your duke-ish tendencies."

Lucy laughed. "It's all coming together perfectly, isn't it?"

"I think so. I'm not so certain you are convinced at your own words, but you shall be. As soon as you enter our first ball, you will remember all your old ambition."

Lucy didn't respond, but she found it curious that Charity would phrase things as she had. Her old ambition? Was it so obvious that her drive to rise to the top was waning? She nearly stumbled. Was it waning?

The sinking sun, the lovely shades of pink and orange in the sky, the warm evening air, all combined to put her at ease. And she was able to sleep that evening just as she'd predicted. Except for one slight disturbance.

The presence of her horse, Firestone, in her dreams. And one handsome stable hand.

12

The next morning, Lucy and the Duchess of Sussex
were invited to tea with the Duchess of Stratton,
Lord Fellon's mother. Charity was not inclined to
attend, and Lucy suspected she had her own social agenda for
the morning. She'd been whistling and skipping around, had a
sensible hairstyle, and was otherwise acting in all ways like
she was about to start a revolution.

But Lucy kissed her cheek, wishing her well. "In whatever
nefarious manner, I wish you success."

Charity laughed but gave no details.

They arrived at tea, Lucy wearing her best morning dress.
The front parlor of the Duchess of Stratton's home was lovely.
Perhaps even lovelier than that of the Duchess of Sussex. A
pale yellow curtain flowed in the delicious breeze that invited
a faint scent of roses. Lucy was immediately put at ease.

"Please be seated, my esteemed guests." The Duchess of
Stratton was a rather large woman. She didn't seem overly
soft. It was more a tough, roguish-looking girth, and Lucy
wondered at her heritage. But when she spoke, it was with the

softest tones. Lucy laughed inside to think what Charity would do with the apparent contradictions in the woman.

Lucy, for one, was charmed. "Thank you for having us, Your Grace."

"I hope you don't mind that it is just us. I decided against including others. Some things are better between more intimate friends." She smiled.

And Lucy warmed under her praise. To be considered an intimate friend of the duchess could only bode well for her and her chances. She held herself perfectly rigid in posture, careful with her sips and limiting her bites to small portions. Nothing would distract her from this opportunity.

After a successful conversation about the weather and the paintings on display at the museum, a servant entered the room. "Lord Fellon, Lord Kenworthy, Your Grace."

"Oh, delightful. Very good. My son."

Lucy's curtsey was deep and respectful, her smile demure. The hand that she placed in his was cradled by him, and his kiss lingered. All good signs, in her opinion.

And then Lord Kenworthy as well performed with perfunctory attentiveness, in the same manner as Lord Fellon, which threw Lucy in a whirl of uncertainty. Perhaps there was no real preference on Lord Fellon's part, not if every lord behaved the same.

But then Lord Fellon sat at her side, close, almost touching, and his eyes never left her face. Once the niceties were covered and the women were engaging Lord Kenworthy in conversation, he lifted her hand in his again. "I should like to promenade this afternoon with the hope that you will join me. Might I pick you up in my phaeton?"

Pleasure filled her. "Yes, I'd be delighted."

"Excellent. I'm pleased to see you here. Mother highly

approves." His eyes held secrets. But not the kind that seemed to fascinate and engage, more the confusing kind that refused to reveal important details that might aid in her deciphering what to say next.

"I have found her to be a friend indeed."

Lord Kenworthy laughed louder than anyone in the room had spoken. And then when the conversations had paused and they were all looking at him, he grinned. "I'm hoping that we will see you ladies at the Kenworthy ball?" He adjusted his sleeves. "I believe Mother included you and your sister, Miss Charity, on the invitation."

Lucy looked to her grace who nodded. "Most certainly. We responded we would attend."

"And that is tomorrow evening." Lord Fellon smiled. "My otherwise tedious week has just brightened up considerably."

She smiled, inwardly thrilled at her progress.

"Might I have the first set?"

"I would save it for no one but you."

"It is our tradition at this point, I believe."

"Certainly."

"Then I'd like the supper set as well if you'll oblige me? Perhaps an increase in tradition?" His words were pretty, his eyes sincere, but something about him also seemed…bored. But then everyone in the ton seemed bored. From what she could tell, it was good ton to be mostly bored with anything and everything.

"I will save you that set as well and a spot at dinner. You do me a great honor."

"Thank you."

The time grew late. She knew it was about past time for them to depart. But she wasn't certain how to go about things.

The Duchess of Sussex clucked. "We've enjoyed

ourselves so much, I look to the hour with regret. But I believe it is time."

And Lucy's respect for the woman grew. She would need the same amount of ease and cleverness in conversation were she to become a duchess.

Everyone in the room stood. When Lord Fellon bowed over her hand, he then tucked it in the crook of his arm as he walked her to the door. "I'll be by this afternoon. The weather should be pleasant if it behaves as it has over the past two days."

"Thank you, I'll look forward to seeing you again." She smiled up into his face, and for a moment, there was a look of enjoyment in his eyes as his gaze travelled over her features. Then he dipped his head and handed her up into the awaiting carriage.

As soon as the duchess had alighted and the door shut, Lucy breathed out in a puff and relaxed her shoulders. But then sat up again, recognizing that she was still in the presence of a duchess. And besides, if she wished to be a duchess, the manners required must become a part of who she was on the inside.

"Oh, please relax." Her grace laughed. "You did well. He seems well and truly interested. And did I hear correctly that he will be singling you out at the ball?"

"Yes, and coming to take me for a ride in his phaeton this afternoon."

"Oh, that *is* something." Her smile was confident, and Lucy loved her even more. "Now, you must get him talking about things he enjoys. He will leave the conversation most enlightened and feeling as though you are a gifted conversationalist even if he is the only person speaking."

Lucy smiled. "I shall do my best. Typically, I find that he is mostly bored."

"I discovered details from his mother." Her conspiratorial tone excited Lucy.

"Oh?"

"Yes, if you wish to get him talking in an animated fashion, ask him about his horse, the training for it, the height of his jumps, that sort of thing."

Should be easy enough for Lucy. "Excellent, for I too will enjoy that conversation." If only she had Firestone with her in London. Every day would be better with her beloved horse.

"Oh tosh. It doesn't matter if you enjoy the conversation. But most certainly listen with rapt attention even if you wish to be hearing any other subject, for there is nothing a man loves more than a woman who dotes on his every word."

Lucy added the woman's sage advice to all the other things she catalogued in her brain about how to be the perfect duchess.

When they arrived back in front of the home, a carriage was just leaving. "I wonder what she's been up to." The Duchess of Sussex studied the back of the departing carriage but said nothing more.

Then another pulled up. "Goodness me." Her grace put a hand on Lucy's arm, and they walked into the house just as a group of women and one man were approaching the doors to exit.

When they saw the duchess, they stepped back immediately, and all curtseyed or bowed, depending.

"Pardon me, Your Grace." The man in the group rose from his bow to seek his pardon.

"Naturally. You're that Lockhart boy, aren't you?"

"I certainly am, ma'am. Though I have grown somewhat

since the last time we've crossed paths." His apologetic rebuke to the duchess nearly brought a laugh, but Lucy kept her twitching lips closed.

His hair fell in his face which he quickly brushed aside. His warm brown eyes were cheerful and intelligent, and there was just something delightfully awkward about him.

"Indeed, you have grown. I supposed you'd like me to call you a man now that you are one."

"I would not complain, but if a boy I must remain, I shall try to bear it well."

"Oh tosh. Certainly, you are Lord Lockhart if anything else."

"Your Grace, you do me honor by remembering."

The rest of their group watched the interchange between the two with great interest. At this point, the duchess continued again to enter her own home. "If you are leaving, best be about it, if you're staying, perhaps we shall not linger in the doorway?"

Charity stepped forward from behind Lord Lockhart. "Your Grace. It is good to see you."

"And you as well, Charity. You will follow me into the front parlor. Come, Lucy."

"Yes, Your Grace." Lucy and Charity dipped a quick curtsey and then left the others to find their way out.

As soon as the door closed behind them, the duchess grinned. "Oh, good show, Charity, good show. That Lord Lockhart is worth ten times of just about any other man in London."

Charity's mouth dropped. And she didn't close it until Lucy kicked her. "Lord Lockhart? That awkward know-it-all who tried to tell me that Tories and Whigs are more alike than people realize? That Lord Lockhart?"

"I imagine so as he was the only Lord Lockhart here, is the only Lord Lockhart that I know of in all of London."

Charity seemed for a moment to be entirely without words. "I..." She closed her mouth and sat in the nearest chair.

Lucy and her grace sat as well, both watching Charity struggle for words. Lucy knew that the Duchess of Sussex couldn't possibly know how odd it was for Charity to be without words, but all the same, she seemed as baffled as Lucy.

At last, Charity just shook her head. "I have no interest in Lord Lockhart...at all. I admit it was good of him to come to my...your home. He made a rather different-looking suffragist."

"A what?" Lucy's grin widened. "You had a meeting about votes for women, and he came?"

"Yes, and I admit that was very forward thinking of him, but he can't really be sincere." She frowned. "Though he did seem sincere, and all the flyers he made, those seemed like sincerely made flyers." She dropped her head into her hand. "I don't know what he thinks he is doing, but I have no designs on the man. I barely know him." Charity's face turned the brightest red, and Lucy wasn't certain what to think of this development. But she wished more than anything that another of their sisters was present to share the first blush of new love on Charity's face with her.

Kate was in town. They would visit Katie tomorrow, and she would help Lucy get the full story out of Charity.

"Well, certainly these things must progress naturally, but never fear, Charity. He seems as ready to marry you as any man."

"Marry?" Charity paused for a moment with glazed eyes

staring at something far away, or at least something not usual in Charity's life. But then she focused again and asked, "How was your visit to the duchess?"

"It was lovely. Your sister is quite the favorite. In fact." She stood and rushed to the door. "Come. We must prepare you for the ride in the park."

"Ride?" Charity looked from one to the other.

"Yes, Lord Fellon is coming to take me out in his phaeton."

"And you must prepare for such a thing?" Charity looked as though she might say more but then just followed Lucy out the parlor room door and up the stairs.

When the duchess was out of earshot, things felt more companionable between them. "So it was a good visit then?"

"It was excellent. The duchess supports me, I believe. And Lord Fellon gave every indication that he would be pursuing me. I've got the first and supper sets for the Kenworthy ball tomorrow night."

"What is this ball?"

"Oh yes, you're invited too. Lord Kenworthy is a perfectly amiable, jolly sort of man you might be happy to know."

"I think I should like a ball."

Lucy watched her for any sign of humor in her statement, but it looked as though she were serious. How intriguing. Her sister wanted to go to a ball. "How was your meeting? And who is this Lord Lockhart? Was your meeting not about women's things? Suffrage and other issues?"

"Yes, but men are invited. They should be involved. None of this will pass unless men support our cause." She huffed a little bit as they entered Lucy's room. "And why shouldn't they be involved? More of them should start attending these meetings. In my opinion, a man is only worth anything if he sees the value in a woman's voice. If he can see that women should be educated."

"And does Lord Lockhart?" Lucy tried to sound as nonchalant as possible, but the question was pretty pointed and there was no hiding her interest in Charity's thoughts on Lord Lockhart.

But instead of balking at the intrusive nature of her questions, Charity seemed preoccupied with her own reactions. "That man is infuriating. He comes, but then he spouts off his opinions about things. And sometimes, women just want to talk about the things that affect us without some man explaining it to us, you know?"

"But I thought you said he was supportive."

She huffed again. "He is."

"Then I don't understand…"

Charity flopped down on Lucy's bed. "He just needs to stop being right all the time." Her frown grew. Then she rolled over onto her stomach. "But let's talk about you. I know you aren't June and your situation is different, but it seems like you've had this wonderful morning with your hopeful's mother and he is paying you attention." She waited.

Lucy wasn't sure what Charity was looking for, but she nodded. "Yes, things are moving forward exactly as I'd hoped." She knew they would be. Or at least she'd hoped they would. Things were in line. The duchesses were supportive. With that one hurdle seemingly easier to cross than she'd thought, she saw no reason why she would not be married to the man.

"You say that as though you are discussing the weather. You sounded more excited about your *gowns*, honestly." Charity narrowed her eyes.

"Don't underestimate the enjoyment of a new gown." She

laughed, but when Charity would not be diverted, she frowned. "I don't know what you want from me, but that's how I am about things. You know I don't get giddy like Grace or even emotional like June. I'm basically nothing like Kate. I'm going about this the way I do anything." She shook her head. "No. Not like the way you ride."

Lucy's smile came without warning. "Oh, I love to ride. I miss my horse."

Charity snorted. "If you could marry a horse, you'd be happiest of all."

Or the stable hand. The words entered her mind with a force of their own, causing a shocked choking sound in her throat and an immediate redness to her face. She waved a hand at her cheeks. "Goodness. What on earth. No, Charity. I will not be marrying my horse." She laughed. "But I'll be pleased as pie to have a stable full of them if I like." She plopped down next to Charity on the bed. "I'm not in this for a love match, but there are benefits, are there not?"

"Yes, I suppose there are." They laid together on their backs staring up at the ceiling. "But can you be happy with such a life?"

She breathed twice before she nodded. "Yes, I believe I can." Would it be the anxious, heart-pounding feelings she had when talking to Mr. Sullivan? No. But that was just fine. Those feelings weren't entirely pleasant anyway.

For what seemed like the hundredth time since she'd left home, she told herself to stop thinking about Mr. Sullivan.

"I'm behind you no matter what you decide. The Standish Sisters of Sussex are a force for certain, and we will do whatever you need."

Lucy turned to face her, their noses close enough she could count the flecks of gold in Charity's eyes. "And for that,

I will be happy forever. What more do I need than a family full to the brim with love and happiness?"

They talked of memories, of their parents and the poorer times, with fondness for as long as they could, until Lucy's maid came knocking with instructions from the duchess to prepare herself for her ride in the park.

Charity stood, grumbling. "Prepare yourself so that you might ride in the wind and muss yourself all up again?"

But Lucy just laughed and shooed her out. She found she was quite looking forward to this outing. And nothing Charity grumbled about could change her happy anticipation.

13

W hen Lord Fellon arrived at the front step, Lucy was ready and stepped outside with him before he could come inside.

He reached out his hand. "You look lovely."

"Thank you. It is such a lovely day. I admit to looking forward to this outing above all others."

"Do you enjoy riding in the park? Or is it the company?" His eyes sparkled, and she grinned at his first attempt at flirting. He'd always been friendly, of course. But this felt different.

She lowered her lashes and allowed him to help her up into the phaeton. Then she smiled as he sat beside her. "The company, of course."

He nodded. "Just so. I quite agree with you there." He lifted the reins, and the horse moved at the barest suggestion.

"But I love horses. And the thought of riding just like this in such beautiful weather makes me happier than most anything."

"And now I shall be equally happy." He seemed relaxed,

and much of the formality that seemed to govern his efforts lifted.

"Do you also enjoy horses? Yours are excellent."

"I enjoy them above most else. My father and I are working on a stable. We have direct bloodlines of four champion horses."

"That's incredible. What a wonderful boon."

"And a lot of work and research. We have dreamed of this for most of my life." He talked for many minutes of the boyhood days of dreaming of owning his own stables of racehorses or breeding them. "And I have just come across the most valuable piece of information."

"Oh?" She smiled. And the duchess was right. He glowed under the attention and seemed to gain energy the more he spoke.

"Yes, I've learned of Prinny's new stable hands. He's finally convinced them to work at the Royal Pavilion stables. They are actually quite accomplished on their own and would only work, for royalty, mind you, if Prinny agreed to let them go after a certain time and if he also let them continue to build their business."

Lucy's mouth dropped. Was he talking about the Sullivans? Or did the prince have this arrangement with another stable hand?

"In fact, you must know them, or perhaps you don't. But they apparently also keep the horses of their original family stables and insist upon maintaining the smaller stables as well." He seemed bemused. "Loyal servants if I've ever heard of any. Because at this point, they've established themselves in the trade. They are well on their way to being landholders." Lord Fellon turned to her. "Quite remarkable, really."

"Indeed." Her mind was spinning. She could hardly think. "And what is the boon for you?"

"Oh, forgive me. I got so caught up in their story. They have agreed to consult with Father and I. It was difficult to find an appointment time, we have been reaching out for months. But turns out, the son is on his way to London, today, I believe, and has agreed to come calling tomorrow. I must say I'm most excited. I have a book full of questions to ask him."

"Excellent. And you feel that he will help you on your way to your dream stable."

"I do indeed. I'd try to hire the man myself if I believed I could get him. But the prince has exclusivity, and once he's finished in Brighton, I daresay he won't be working for any noble. The man will have set himself up nicely to become a gentleman."

The air Lucy was holding came out faster than she had prepared. "Goodness!"

"Exactly. How often does something like this happen? But they've been consulting with gentlemen for years. I've heard tell of their excellent advice, even for horse betting tips, time and again. And now that they are associated with the prince, well, I'm just pleased I had already been in contact to set up the appointment."

"Very fortunate, certainly. I'd love to see your horses some time."

"Would you? Do we share this interest in common?"

"Yes, most definitely."

"Then perhaps not tomorrow as we have the ball, but the day after?"

"That would be lovely, thank you."

"I agree." They entered the paths on the park. And

everyone seemed to be out with the same idea. They stopped their phaeton more than they moved, but Lucy was too distracted for much conversation anyway. The friendly waves and general topics of weather were perfect for her state of inner turmoil. Mr. Sullivan. In London. Today?

The news of his rise in society wasn't entirely new to her, but the thought that someone so elevated would consider Mr. Sullivan's story to be a rise in stations was profoundly affecting Lucy's ability to breathe as well as think. She caught herself forcing a long, deep breath now and again, and her hands held tightly clasped. But those were all the evidences she hoped were visible to give clues to her current state of being. Mr. Sullivan in London.

She didn't quite know what to think. Mr. Sullivan in London, talking with Lord Fellon? As she smiled and waved and acknowledged Lord Fellon's acquaintances and some of her own, her thoughts wrapped around those words and weaved in and out of them, tasting and testing them against her world.

As yet, she had found no comfortable arrangement of roles and placement of people and relationships.

"Are you even hearing me at all?" Lord Fellon laughed, but his voice had an unfamiliar edge to it.

"What? Of course. I guess that last little bit blew away in the wind." She leaned closer to him and forced herself to drink in every word the man said. But she couldn't change the turmoil inside.

By the time Lord Fellon had left her at home once again, she was exhausted. Every point of feeling in her was on high alert. Just the act of brushing her fingers against the wall was more than she could bear. The banister felt uncomfortably scratchy. Her feet felt every uneven plane of wood under her slippers. And all of a sudden, more than anything, she wished to take out every pin.

Charity appeared at the top of the stairs.

"I need to lie down."

Her maid was summoned, her hair loosened, and her stays removed. She pulled the covers up to her chin and closed her eyes.

Charity and the duchess were both thinking she was suddenly ill, but Lucy was simply unsure what to do and how to behave. No duchess had to figure out such a dilemma of emotion. Of course, she was better off with Lord Fellon. Every woman in the ton would be the most fortunate woman of this season to have his attention. But suddenly, the idea of Mr. Sullivan. A rising gentleman? A landowner? Her stable hand visiting with Lord Fellon? Lord Fellon respected his opinions? He was in high demand among the lords?

The question that repeated itself over and over in her mind, that allowed her to rest but kept sleep at bay, was certainly persistent.

Why again was it so important that she marry a man of title?

She spent the night tossing and turning, finding no answers drifting among the tumble of thoughts.

When she'd just about given up on sleep ever again in her life, Charity burst through the door. "I know you're awake."

"Yes." It was morning, certainly, but she hadn't yet had the energy to rise and get dressed or even summon a tray of breakfast.

"You're going to want to get up for this."

She sat up immediately at her sister's excited tone.

Charity stood at the window which overlooked the front drive and waved her over.

Lucy rose, throwing back her covers with a vengeance, the enemies of her relaxation, as they'd given no comfort, no rest whatsoever.

She plodded to the window, peering down at the drive below. "Is that?" *Firestone.* She pressed her forehead to the glass. *Her horse.* And Mr. Sullivan riding atop as comfortable as day. Happiness filled her. Whether for Mr. Sullivan or her horse, she did not attempt to decipher, but she turned to run from the room, only barely stopping in time as Charity shouted, "No!"

"What?" She turned, out of breath already.

"You are not dressed." Charity shook her head.

Lucy looked down at her shift. "Oh bother."

And then Charity laughed.

"What?" Lucy frowned.

"I've never seen you, not once in your new title-focused life, be bothered by holding to propriety."

"Wave at him. Tell him to stay."

Charity waved and held up a finger. "He nodded. He's not going anywhere. The man came up from Brighton to bring you your horse. He's gonna wait around for the reward." She laughed again.

"And what is the reward?"

Her maid entered. "Oh, Susan, please. Throw something on me. I don't care what." As the maid turned away, she called, "Wait, something blue."

"Yes, miss."

Lucy rushed to her dressing table, and Charity came to stand beside her. When she placed hands on her shoulders, Lucy looked up to meet her eyes in the mirror.

Charity's face, instead of mocking amusement, held a large amount of compassion. "You are free, you know."

"Free?" Lucy studied her sister's face.

"If he's your first choice."

Something akin to alarm barreled through her, adding to the already angst-filled heart pain. "No. No. Charity. It's Firestone. He brought me my horse. I spent the day yesterday talking of nothing but horses, and I needed her. He brought her."

"Hmm."

"Because it's his job. He's hired to take care of our horses."

"Not really anymore. And I don't think he's hired to ride them all the way up here from Brighton. And why aren't you freaking out that someone else is on your horse?"

Lucy stopped. "True. I'm not, am I?" Up until that moment, she'd really only let a precious few people ride Firestone. She slumped. "You don't think I'm losing my sense, do you?"

Charity laughed again. "You might be. But for all the best reasons."

"You speak in riddles. I suppose you think I'm inappropriately attracted to the stable hand." The words shook her to say, to think. Because of course she wasn't. Nothing could be more ridiculous. But she was certainly distracted. "Truly, Charity. This excitement is almost entirely focused on my horse. And on the fact that I am going riding."

"Oh dear." Susan nearly dropped the blue morning dress. "Would you like your riding habit?"

"No, no, not yet. I need to prepare for the ball soon. I'll just be a moment."

"Yes, miss." She hurried and dressed Lucy, only just barely tying her hair back in a low bun before Lucy ran down the stairs and out the front door.

Mr. Sullivan had dismounted from Firestone and stood at her side, reins in hand. His whole manner of dress seemed to have changed. He was dressed to ride but in finer clothes than she ever saw around their stables. He wore a cravat. He looked, for all intents and purposes, like a well-dressed gentleman and not a groomsman. Which, she had to remind herself, perhaps he no longer was? Not officially, but a royally appointed horse expert? She wasn't entirely sure what their arrangement had become.

His eyes sparkled at her, but his face seemed aloof, if anything. "Miss Lucy." He bowed.

"Mr. Sullivan." She stepped closer. "I cannot express how much this means to me. That you would do this, bring my horse?" She had to stop, as she thought for a moment she might create some tears. How utterly ridiculous.

She reached a hand up to Firestone's soft nose. And her beloved mare nickered. "Hey, girl. I missed you."

When she turned to the still quiet Mr. Sullivan, her mouth open to pour out gratitude, he at last responded. "Lord Morley asked me to bring Firestone."

"Oh, of course."

"And I was happy to do so. I am here in London on business. A favor to my former employer is the least I could do."

She nodded slowly. "I am not up to date on your goings and comings."

"We are overseeing the stables at the castle. How could we not? They have been in our family longer than yours."

She bristled. "Perhaps. Perhaps not."

He dipped his head. "Because of our connection there and long-time loyalty, there will be others in our employ who actually maintain the horses and serve the family."

"Yes, I think you said something like that back at the castle, didn't you?"

"We probably did, yes. It was our plan to negotiate with the prince just such a situation."

He seemed distant. His eyes told her one thing, that he was pleased to see her, but his aloof tone and attention said something completely different.

She stared into his eyes. He had not once looked to the ground in his typical servant's submissive expression. "Mr. Sullivan? What's different?"

"Nothing. Everything." He smiled. And for a moment, she saw the Mr. Sullivan she knew. "Things are changing for our family. Everything we were talking about, the opportunities with the prince, our new business, all of it. It's all coming together. I'm meeting with a lord today. A future duke."

"That's excellent."

"In fact, I need to go."

"Oh, certainly."

"Where do you want me to put Firestone?"

"I'll have to ask the duchess... I don't know."

"She has stables?"

"I believe so?"

He handed her the reins. "Excellent. Then here you go."

Then he turned and walked down the drive and turned the corner out of sight.

Firestone nickered at her again.

While Lucy patted her horse absentmindedly, she tried to figure out what she thought about this new Mr. Sullivan. Not a servant? Who was he, then?

She stood in front of the house for a time, until Firestone bumped her arm.

"Oh, sorry, girl. Now what?" She laughed.

Then she walked up the front stairs, horse in hand. At her knock, the butler answered and to his credit did not even blink an eye before he asked, "Would you like this horse to be placed in our stables, miss?"

"Oh yes, do we have stables?"

"Certainly. A fine building, with the horses for the carriage. But I'm certain this new beauty will be comfortable."

"Thank you. Yes, I'd like that."

A footman arrived and took the reins.

"I'll see you soon, my beauty."

When she went back into the house, she felt more confused than ever. She had to prepare for the ball when all she really wanted was to be on her horse.

And, she admitted, she wanted to think about Mr. Sullivan some more.

14

L ucy and Charity entered the Kenworthy home arm in arm with the Duchess of Sussex at their side. After greeting Lord Kenworthy and his parents, they approached the entrance to the grand ballroom. "The Duchess of Sussex. Miss Charity Standish. Miss Lucy Standish." They were announced to a room full of some of the most elite in all of London. When they stepped into the room, the Duchess of York gestured for them to join her in conversation. Royals, nobles, gentlemen, all looking in their direction.

"And here we are," Lucy breathed out, squeezing Charity's arm.

"I see them. And besides that group in the back corner over there, I see no one better than anyone else we know, and…" She leaned closer. "No one better than a Standish, and that's for certain."

Lucy laughed. "I can agree with you there. I do miss our sisters. Has Kate come to London yet?"

"They were delayed in Brighton." Charity made a point of

looking out over the room. "You're right. Here we are. Is all this everything you'd hoped for?"

Lucy knew she was teasing her, knew her sister was enjoying herself in her own way; had she not said she'd like to go to a ball? But instead of helping to set her at ease, Charity's question stung for some reason.

"We've been to balls before," her sister added. "Brighton has plenty of balls."

"Charity. I can be pleased we have finally arrived in the eyes of the bon ton if I want to. Look at all these people. Look at us in our brand-new gowns. Remember when we used to count our coins? Remember when we couldn't afford to buy meat?"

"Oh hush. Yes, I remember. I'm teasing you, and I well remember all of it." She surprised Lucy with a quick kiss on the cheek. "Now come. Let's enjoy this ball as two people who well know how to appreciate it."

"Agreed."

The Duchess of York stood as they approached. "Well now, let me take a look at you both." She held her hands out and proclaimed them both lovely.

As they moved away, leaving the Duchess of York with the other duchess, they approached a group of women they'd met before.

"And here they are." Lady Dorothy lifted her lips in what might have been a smile if she were actually pleased.

"Hello." Lucy and Charity curtseyed to the others and to Lady Dorothy, though Lucy could not forget the role she played in nearly ruining June's every happiness. She'd aided and assisted in the deceptions. Lucy inwardly cringed at the thought. But the others seemed pleasant enough, and when the music began, Lord Fellon approached for their set.

The other ladies curtseyed and simpered and fluttered eyelashes, but Lord Kenworthy bowed before Charity. "Might I have this dance?"

"Yes, certainly." Charity put her hand on his arm, and the two sisters stepped out onto the ballroom floor together.

When they stood together in their foursome, Lord Kenworthy laughed to Lord Fellon. "I don't believe I've been introduced to my lovely dance partner."

"Oh certainly. This is Miss Charity Standish. And this is Lord Kenworthy."

Charity smiled. "Pleased to meet you."

They all curtseyed and bowed to one another as part of the upcoming set.

"This ball will be monstrously dull, I'm afraid." Lord Fellon yawned to Lord Kenworthy. He hadn't yet said a word to Lucy, besides to retrieve her for their dance.

She circled round him as the dance dictated. "I thought you talked of it as a great diversion. You are largely why I have come." She smiled, trying to soften words that she realized now were more bold than she would have liked.

"Right. Yes. We must put up appearances at any rate, mustn't we?"

She tilted her head in confusion, but he moved on to the next lady and circled round her before returning to Lucy.

Lord Kenworthy indicated something with his chin, and Lord Fellon followed his gaze. The two snickered together while Lucy and Charity were left wondering from what they were blatantly excluded.

A woman stood at the side of the dance floor alone.

A deep concern rose inside Lucy as her suspicions grew that the men were laughing at her, and most likely because she was alone. Her suspicions were confirmed when she heard the word "wallflower."

When the four of them stood together again, Charity turned to Lord Kenworthy. "For a man who hopes to woo my sister, Lord Fellon has paid precious little attention to her in this dance, do you agree?"

Lord Kenworthy opened his mouth and then closed it again before sharing a glance with Lord Fellon. Then both laughed together.

And Lucy began to suspect they were a bit in their cups.

But then Lord Fellon turned to Lucy. "I have not been as attentive, no. If I have offended you in any way, I apologize. Perhaps I might make it up to you this week when I come calling?"

"Of course. And I have not been left wanting. We're all dancing together, and with the others, I've had plenty of conversation."

"Excellent." Lord Fellon nodded and then turned back to Lord Kenworthy.

By the time the set was over, Lucy was glad of it. If she had not her sister, she'd have spoken precious few words at all. But because Charity was beside her, she also had felt the need to explain away the lords' behavior, to be embarrassed by it, and to be more affected by it than she would otherwise have been.

Was she to be ignored for most of her life? Considered less important than a friend nearby? She shouldn't have let her thoughts go there. For how could she go about her business of marrying Lord Fellon if she were thinking so ill of him? But Charity brought out the self-respecting independent side to her nature, and she had to admit that Lord Fellon's treatment of her left much to be desired.

Perhaps she was just tired. Fatigued so early in the evening did not bode well for her. But what did duchesses do when they were tired? They behaved with the utmost charm and decorum.

And they probably went home whenever they liked.

But since she didn't have that luxury, she would have to continue on as she was.

When the dance finished and the lords left Charity and Lucy to themselves, she turned to her sister in exasperation.

"That was the worst dance I've had." Charity shook her head. "Is he always thus?"

"Thus? What specifically?"

"So utterly and completely overlooking you? Did he speak five words to you?"

"Yes. But just five." Lucy laughed, though she didn't find much of the conversation truly humorous. "I don't know what has come over him. Perhaps it is the influence of Lord Kenworthy. He's typically polite, well-mannered, and attentive."

"But certainly not in raptures."

"No, but he and I are not to have a love match. I believe we get on well enough together, or at least, I used to think so."

"Praise all the dance faeries if you're able to see where you deserve better."

"Consider it might be a sacrifice worth taking."

Charity opened her mouth and closed it again three times before a sound would exit her lips. And Lucy might not ever know what she was about to say because of all the people to make an appearance, the new Lord Lockhart bowed before her and asked her to dance.

Lucy watched them. Charity was alive with laughter, and his eyes never left her. They conversed for all of the set.

Someone came to claim Lucy for the next set, and Lord Lockhart and Charity were on their way to the women in the corner who Charity had pointed out as quality associations of all in the room.

As Lucy whirled around and then skipped to one side and another, she wanted to applaud Charity. Her sister stood near the wallflower, engaged her in conversation, and then walked with her anew in the direction of the others.

Lucy couldn't be more proud.

When Lord Fellon came to claim her for another set, she was well and truly ready to return home. But she pasted on a smile and danced the longest reel of her life.

As she shimmied down the center of the two lines of dancers, she realized she should be ecstatic, watching all her dreams come true before her eyes. But she was feeling only mild amusement, the smallest bit of pleasure, and a great amount of discomfort.

The ball continued with more of the same. Lord Fellon was more attentive. He came to find her for their final set with a warm smile. The hand that held hers cradled her fingers as though she were important to him. When he pulled her closer for the waltz, his eyes searched her face. "You are lovely."

She sucked in her breath. How did a duchess respond to such a compliment? She dared herself not to blush, but her cheeks warmed. Then she smiled. "Thank you. I enjoy our time together. Tell me, have you gone riding recently?"

"Certainly. I ride every morning with some of the men from Cambridge."

"What an excellent idea. I should like—"

"But we needn't discuss horses at the ball."

"We needn't?" She'd been just about to tell him all about

Firestone and how she'd very much like to go riding with him sometime.

"No." He placed his hand above their heads to meet hers. Then they moved to the side. "You look such a pretty picture in this gown. I'm distracted by it, by you." His eyes had an appreciative gleam. Was this how it felt to be complimented by one who admired you?

She wasn't feeling particularly warm.

His gaze travelled over her skin in a proprietary manner, as if he already owned her or wished to.

Lucy almost shifted away under his fingers but by a force of will kept herself dancing. His hand pulled her closer.

He smelled nice, a mix of cloves and sandalwood. But his hands were strong, his face hungry, and his breath stale.

And Lucy wanted more than anything to step away. As she was about to cry a need for a lemonade, the chords for the music to make an end sounded, and she breathed out in relief.

"Disappointed that our waltz is over too soon?" His smile was sympathetic, almost patronizing. And for some reason, his whole presence felt like someone's hand on goosefleshpuckered skin, queasy and unpleasant.

She kept her hand on his arm in the most proper of distances, but he eased closer, tucked her into his side, and placed another hand over top hers.

Perhaps all of these were good signs that he was interested in pursuing her, but she could only feel encroached upon and, if she were being honest with herself, caged.

Is this what it would feel like to be married to someone you didn't love? What if she didn't want to sit close or feel his arm around her? The thought of kissing the man sounded... unpleasant. Oh dear.

All through dinner, she smiled through his attentions,

which were many. His hand reached for hers under the table. His boot scooted closer so that their feet touched, her skirts brushing up against his breeches.

Then during dessert, he held up a fork.

"Hm?" She smiled.

"Try this."

She laughed. "I've just eaten all of mine. It was delicious."

"Ah, but see, it tastes better when eaten from my fork."

She swallowed, not daring to look at those around her who would surely be watching. Did duchesses eat off the forks of others in public? She didn't know. But she knew one thing. If she didn't please this lord, she would not become a duchess at all. And so she giggled. It sounded more like a forced ratchet sound, but he seemed pleased by it at any rate.

Then she leaned forward and opened her mouth.

When he placed the forkful of food inside, he ran the fork along her lip for a moment. She closed her mouth and forced a swallow of the pudding. "Mm." She smiled. "It does taste better coming from you."

And she felt so unlike herself that she could almost no longer stomach the evening. What had happened to her usual constant commitment to propriety, to behaving as a duchess? What did one do when pleasing a lord meant behaving in a manner foreign to one's inclinations or even propriety?

Charity's voice carried over to them from down the table.

As usual, she sat surrounded by men, and all were in deep conversation. They spoke over one another and jumped off each other's thoughts. And Charity had never seemed happier.

"Your sister would do well to mind her tongue." Lord Fellon's voice in her ear made her jump.

"Oh! I'm sorry. You startled me." She eyed her sister

again and then the expressions of others at the table. Most seemed to be not paying them any mind. But there were some disapproving expressions as well.

She sought out the Duchess of Sussex. She seemed perfectly comfortable, at least from outward appearances. The Duchess of York seemed intrigued by the conversation. Lucy almost laughed but then remembered that Lord Fellon had expressed his disapproval.

He leaned closer. "I appreciate your ease of conversation. And that you don't become caught up on the same mannerisms as your sister."

She turned to him. Their eyes were close. His were sincere and a touch superior in expression, the kind of look that Charity could never abide. She and he would not get along well, to be sure. But there were not many with whom Charity would get on well. She was nontraditional, to say the least.

Lucy smiled. And she loved her for it. Thinking of the wallflower, she had to concede that perhaps when all was said and done, they should all be a bit more like Charity. If they were free to do so. Lucy must be the one to win over their firm place in society forever.

"Thank you, Lord Fellon. We are of different temperaments and interests. She chooses her circles carefully, and I mine."

He reached for her hand and then kept it in his.

No one seemed to be paying them any mind. So she tried to relax and enjoy this very obvious indication of his preference for her.

After dinner, they danced one more set together, Charity danced two more with Lord Lockhart, and at last, after what seemed like the longest ball of Lucy's life, they sat in the carriage with the duchess to return home.

"What a success." Her grace clapped her hands. "I've never seen Lord Fellon pay such pointed attentions to another. He almost looks as though he might be developing a tendre for you?" She waited for Lucy to confirm her suspicions.

"I believe he is, yes, if his actions are any indication, and he told me I look lovely, multiple times."

"Oh, that is news indeed. I am so pleased. Pleased indeed."

"Thank you, Your Grace."

Charity leaned her head back against the carriage wall behind them, seeming to be lost in thought.

Even though Lucy would like nothing more than to discuss Charity's experience, everyone went straight to bed and Lucy knew she would have to wait until morning or until Charity felt disposed to discuss such things.

And Lucy was left with no one to distract her from a terribly convoluted mess of thoughts. She suspected sleep would not come. And she was right.

15

L ucy awoke to Charity sitting on her bed, reading.
"Hello, sister." She turned to face her.
"At last awake." She huffed and then rested a
hand on Lucy's head. "You had quite the night of it if I could
tell from where I stood."

"Yes. I'm not sure how I feel about that ball."

"I made some new friends, and we might have a few more
male attendees at our next meeting."

"When is it?"

Charity eyed her for a minute. "You asking because you
want to come?"

"I think I do. I need to wash away some of the memories
of last night."

"Was it so terrible?"

"I just don't know how many of those people we saw last
night were our kinds of people. I got tired of them, and more
than once, I was left unsettled. I don't know how a duchess
would respond to Lord Fellon some of the time. I'm not
always certain how to behave. And..." She breathed in

deeply, trying to collect the thoughts that wanted to come pouring out. "And I really don't know if I will like being a duchess all the time, day in and day out."

Charity looked like she wanted to say a million things, and Lucy began to regret bringing her into the conversation at all, but her sister surprised her and said only, "We are having a meeting today, and of course, I've invited some more women over during calling hours."

"I'll be there for calling hours, and Lord Fellon mentioned something about visiting the stables, but I've heard nothing since. I shall come if I can."

Was she feeling rebellious after such a long amount of time feeling censured? Was she responding to Lord Fellon's reprimand of her sister by doing precisely what he disapproved of?

Whatever the reason, she had a newer interest and appreciation for her sister. "I saw what you did for that woman on the side of the ballroom floor."

Charity thought for a minute and then nodded. "For Florence? Oh, she's a gem. She's coming today too. You will enjoy her."

"I've just never been more proud to be a Standish sister."

"Thank you, my dear. You would have done the same if you weren't tied into your quest."

Lucy smiled, but Charity's words sank in. What else would she do if she wasn't tied into her quest? Who else could she help?

"I've started a new book."

Lucy nodded. Charity was always starting a new book.

"But this one I think is going to be the keeper."

"I hope so. When you burned that last one, I think a part of my life flashed before my eyes."

"I do regret that now. There was probably a good sentence or two in some of those pages."

"Hmm. We all thought so." Lucy and the other sisters had read countless things written by Charity that were then destroyed. Perhaps her sister would feel confident enough in something that she would actually submit it somewhere and, like Kate, have regular publications so more could learn from her.

"Let's get up. Have some breakfast, and go for a walk."

"Excellent notion." Lucy rang for Susan. "Perhaps a tray in our rooms?"

"Absolutely."

Lucy wrapped a robe about herself to cut out the chill.

When Susan arrived, she immediately rang for a maid to warm up the fire, and then she gathered the items needed for her to dress for a walk and then for morning callers.

When Charity and she were at last out of doors, Lucy felt considerably better than she had last night. Her life had started to realign with what she'd always thought her life should be. In theory, working and preparing to be a duchess was turning out to be different than the reality. Did she still want that life? She did. More than likely. But last evening was not as enjoyable as others had been.

They stepped out into the park, and the sun came out from behind the clouds, chasing away some of the spring chill.

"A lovely day," Charity observed. "Days like today make me miss our cliffs in Brighton."

"Oh, I as well. There is nothing as beautiful as Brighton in all the world." Lucy sighed.

And Charity looked at her like she'd grown a horn.

"What?"

"You're just… That sounded exactly like Grace or even Kate. But you? Rhapsodizing about the beauties of Brighton?"

"It is beautiful, is it not?"

"Certainly."

"And I can feel free to miss it."

"You most certainly can." Charity shook her head. "Perhaps there's a side to you we've never seen."

"I think I just need to go riding. I'll feel better once I'm up on Firestone again. I always feel more myself after I've been on a horse."

"We can go riding in the morning perhaps."

"Yes, today is rather full already, isn't it?"

As they moved closer to the area near Grosvenor Square, the park filled with more and more people.

"Certainly many out promenading today, aren't there?"

"Yes, quite." Lucy looked about, recognizing some by sight, others were new faces.

"Is that Mr. Sullivan?" Charity pointed across a small expanse of green to a gathering of men, all in cravats, hessians, and top hats.

"Surely not. I don't see how it could be." She squinted. "Though that one there on the left."

"Yes, him. I think it's the spitting image."

"Do you suppose he is still in London?"

"Probably. Wasn't his meeting with Lord Fellon only just yesterday?"

"I don't remember. I confess I've given it little thought."

The closer they walked, the more the man looked like Mr. Sullivan.

And then Lucy couldn't even believe her eyes or her ears when Lord Fellon stepped out from the group and called her over, indicating the man at his left who was indeed Mr. Sullivan.

"Oh, heavenly days."

"What have we here."

"I wish to turn about and return to the house."

"No, come, don't be chicken livered. We must discover what has transpired with our dear Mr. Sullivan." Charity's eyes were full of mischief which Lucy tried to ignore.

"I don't think I'm smart enough, old enough, wise enough for this kind of conversation."

"Oh, don't be silly. Can you not see the humor?"

"It's not as though I fancy either of them, really, but one I desperately want to marry and the other..." What did she feel about Mr. Sullivan?

"And what of Lord Fellon?" Charity laughed when Lucy's mouth dropped open.

"You, sister, are going to get me in all sorts of trouble."

"Well, I'm just not certain what you are going to do with yourself if our Mr. Sullivan is right here in front of us, behaving as though he belongs in society."

"And why shouldn't he?"

"Precisely, why shouldn't he?" Charity's expression challenged Lucy in every way but did not prove to erase the fact that until this past week, Mr. Sullivan was employed at the castle as their servant. Sort of.

"A stable hand, a groomsman, they're a bit above a regular house servant, aren't they?"

They were now too close for Charity to do anything but snort.

Lord Fellon reached a hand out to Lucy and tucked hers in the crook of his arm. "Hello, my dear."

My dear? Lucy's mouth went dry. And Charity's eyebrows

went up, but all Lucy could do was smile in return. And not look at Mr. Sullivan.

"Guess what we have all just discovered, right before we saw you?" Lord Fellon seemed overly pleased with himself.

"I cannot imagine." How Charity kept from bursting from all that laughter she was keeping at bay, Lucy would never know. But when she at last dared look at Mr. Sullivan, his gaze was intense and not as amused as she would have expected. He watched her, and she wasn't exactly certain what he was looking for.

But she did wish to be standing further apart from Lord Fellon and to have the use of both her hands.

Lord Fellon placed his other hand over top Lucy's. "We have just discovered that our Mr. Sullivan here comes from your stables in Brighton. Isn't that extraordinary!"

"Oh, why yes! But how have the two of you, all of you become acquainted?" Lucy's voice had at last returned, her curiosity winning over any awkwardness.

"You will never guess. But I shall tell you. He is the very man I was speaking of when I told you a horse expert had agreed to see me."

"No!" Lucy's amusement had returned. Charity had the right of it. This conversation was proving to be amusing after all. It must be, else it turn to the most difficult.

"Yes. I could not believe it myself when he told me from whence his family had come. And we were just discussing how incredibly knowledgeable he is. He will be in high demand, indeed. There is a horse race Thursday next, and of course, Tattersall's will be a hotbed of purchases and sales with Mr. Sullivan around to guide us."

"Excellent." Lucy smiled. "And how are you, Mr. Sullivan? London treats you well, I trust."

"Very well indeed."

"He is one of the most sought-after men in London at the moment."

"And they've been good enough to advise me on the purchasing of land."

Charity's small gasp drew most of their attention. So she cleared her throat. "Um, so soon? Congratulations are in order."

"I won't be in a position to purchase land for three to five years, but what these gentlemen have been telling me is that I should be announcing my intention because sometimes the sale or transfer of ownership takes some time, and sometimes an owner will need that time to think it over. They have been most helpful in instructing me also on the ways in which to tell if an estate is profitable and so much more."

"Do you wish for an estate? I would have thought you rather preferred a stable and a business of breeding, selling, and racing horses? And training them?" Lucy stared into his eyes until he returned her gaze, but he shrugged. "I think I could have both."

"And with a fortune accruing, this man will be well sought out by the ladies as well." Lord Fellon shook his head. "And to think I have had my own exclusive advice from the man."

"Exclusive is a bit of stretch, don't you think? Since we know he advises Prinny."

"And me." Lucy's voice caught in her throat. What had she just said?

Charity put a hand to her mouth, but Mr. Sullivan just smiled.

"He advises me as well."

"Oh?" Lord Fellon shook his head. "And just how do you have need of Mr. Sullivan's advice?"

"For my horse, for the horses on our estate. I have counselled often with him and find him to be the most knowledgeable on the subject."

"And there you have it. If not for the prince's recommendation, now we know that Mr. Sullivan truly is worthy."

The others laughed, and Lucy had the sense that they were making fun. She would give much to recant her words, but since that was impossible, she just hoped they would go away.

"Miss Lucy might be privy to trade secrets, which is likely what she is referring to. But those were the benefit of those associated with the castle."

"True. There have been Sullivans at the castle for many generations."

"Is that so? Then that is even better news. For we shall have no secrets between us." His voice was for her alone but loud enough for all.

And she could only look away in response.

No one said anything for a moment, and then Charity laughed. "We are here for a promenade. Would anyone care to join to us?"

"Unfortunately, I must meet with Father and the solicitor, but might I call on you again tomorrow?"

"Of course." Lucy smiled up into his face, feeling the eyes of Mr. Sullivan on her while she did it.

He bowed and left a lingering kiss on her hand. "Until then." He winked. "And don't share any trade secrets until I return."

The others drifted away as well, all except for Mr. Sullivan. "Might I walk with you?"

"Certainly. It shall be a relief over every other person." Charity took his one arm which made Lucy take his other.

And everything in her life felt strangely collided.

"My, you are a gentleman. I feel as though you've assumed quite naturally the air that these other lords have." Charity nodded in appreciation.

"Yes, as long as you don't start acting bored about everything, you shall do quite well here." Lucy stepped closer to him. She almost couldn't help it, as if she did nothing at all, they would be as close as could be.

"But what if I *am* bored about everything?" He laughed. "I've never been a part of such mundane conversations."

"I echo that sentiment. Lucy and I were speaking of something similar after being at the ball last night. It was as if we needed to recover from the company."

"Too true." Lucy stepped quietly beside Mr. Sullivan.

"Not to mention Lord Fellon knows nothing about breeding horses. How on earth that man is a head of his own stables is beyond me."

Lucy stiffened beside him. Her loyalty felt tested. "Now, perhaps he knows more than you think, and it would behoove us all to remember that Lord Fellon will be the Duke of Stratton which is undoubtedly why he pays people to know things he doesn't have a need to know for himself."

Mr. Sullivan bowed his head. "He is a lucky man indeed to have such a one defend his honor."

She softened toward him. "And how have you been? Will you really be staying in London all this time?"

"Long enough to aid all these lords in their bets and purchasing? Certainly. Though my real purpose is to find customers and clients for our new business and stables. I am looking for potential horses to add to our breeding program and for others who might wish to utilize our services."

"That's smart thinking there, Mr. Sullivan." Judging by the swish of her skirts, Charity spun to look at Mr. Sullivan.

"Thank you. Father told me not to come home until I have convinced half the ton to work with us."

"Well, you've certainly won over some of the most influential." Lucy was thinking of Lord Fellon.

"Yes, the prince is certainly a wonderful supporter. I'm happy we negotiated the way we did. His influence has already elevated us to the highest circles."

"I see that." Lucy swallowed. So what was Mr. Sullivan now? She'd asked herself that question again and again to no avail.

They passed by a group of ladies, and every one of them had their eye on Mr. Sullivan. The nearest fluttered her eyelashes unabashedly, and he dipped his head.

"Mr. Sullivan."

"Yes?" He turned to her, an amused twinkle in his eye.

"You cannot be flirting with the women here."

"And why not?"

"Yes, why can't he?" Charity leaned forward so that Lucy could see just how amusing she thought the conversation was sounding.

"Well, for one…" Lucy stopped. There really was no reason why he mustn't flirt with them except, she realized, she did not wish it. But that was not a good enough reason to stop Mr. Sullivan from befriending, flirting with, and even wooing any woman in the world.

"If you like, I won't flirt with them in your presence." The twinkle remained, and one corner of his mouth lifted in a playful tug.

"Oh, do as you like." She looked away, ready to walk in the other direction before she had to listen to this insufferable conversation. But did these women know they were flirting with a stable hand? She pressed her lips together so the words would not exit. But in reality, she wondered how he was getting away with it. How were the men treating him as an equal? And how would he be considered a good catch by any woman?

She knew how. He was by far the most handsome man of their acquaintance, that's how.

He stood, broad shouldered, hair slightly mussed, sharp eyes full of humor, and, most of all, bearing a new confidence that Lucy was finding difficult to resist. His head high, his eyes staring into hers, his well-fitting clothes accentuating everything that was handsome about him. And she suspected he knew it. The man oozed confidence and charm.

She could hardly remember the time when she'd watched him muck out the stables. Everything was too unsettling. She was about to suggest that she and Charity turn back when her sister sighed. "At last, just people from home. It's so nice to relax a little bit, isn't it?" She lowered her shoulders and walked slower.

Was it nice? Could she relax? Because right now, she felt anything but relaxed. Every single bit of her was buzzing with awareness. The hand that rested on his arm might never let him go. Warmth travelled all the way to her toes.

What was going on with her? Why did she have this reaction to him?

He turned his face down to hers, and with his large brown eyes focusing solely on her and so close, she didn't think her voice would work when she nodded to what Charity had just said and then tried to swallow.

"Do you agree with your sister? Is it nice to be with those of us from home?" His voice was deep and warm and teasing. But his eyes were earnest. And she knew what he was asking.

In so many ways, he wanted to know if he held a place of intimacy in her life.

"It is nice to see you, Mr. Sullivan. But I admit I'm trying to accustom myself to this new you." She shook her head.

"Do you not like the new me?"

"The new you is wonderful, I'd imagine, for you. This opportunity to grow your stables, to meet others who could help you on your way. To purchase a property." She shrugged. "I'm truly happy for you, Mr. Sullivan." And she was. But as confused as she was happy.

He dipped his head. "Thank you. I'm rather pleased myself."

Charity laughed. "Oh, excuse me a moment." She stepped away toward the fountain. "Don't mind me. I'll be right there. I've been eyeing this water over here. It's lovely."

When she was out of earshot, Mr. Sullivan stepped closer. "I admit to being happiest at seeing you here."

"Are you?" As she looked up into his face, she saw the truth of his words, saw the truth of his admiration.

"I am. I hope that, perhaps, my new standing, my new opportunities might..." He sighed. "I'm speaking too soon. I know these things are done with more subtlety, but I don't know when I'll see you again."

"You can come calling."

"At the duchess's home? I don't know that my situation has improved to that length."

"You could come riding with me, allow me to consult with you about my horses?" She astounded herself at her bravery. Was she arranging a meeting, a rendezvous, with Mr. Sullivan?

"Excellent. When?"

"Tomorrow?"

"I'll be at White's in the afternoon."

"Tomorrow morning then."

"I have the races and then Tattersall's."

"Goodness. I'm busy as well, but I'm arranging things in my mind so that we can meet."

"I do apologize, but I am at the beck and call of others, if you recall."

She sighed. "I do. The day after then."

"Certainly. In the morning. I shall meet you at the stables."

"I'll look forward to it."

Charity approached. "There. Much refreshed." Her hair was wet around her neck, and her fingers were still dripping with water.

"What have you done, sister?"

"I was warm. This feels lovely." She grinned at Mr. Sullivan. "I'd suggest a good old-fashioned water fight with the two of you, but I don't think Miss Lucy would stand for it."

"I most certainly would not." She shook her head. "We are in the most public part of the park. Everyone has walked by or will at one point or another."

"And you concern yourself so much with what they will think." Mr. Sullivan watched her closely.

"Yes, I most certainly do, and you'd be wise to do the same. Considering your standing right now is based solely on the goodwill of others."

"And when I purchase land? Will my standing be reliant upon anything else besides the goodwill of others?"

Lucy considered him and tried to ignore Charity's exultant expression. "I see what you mean. But I cannot afford to lose respectability right now."

"Your duke."

"He's not my duke. And that is precisely the problem."

"And I'll ask you the same question you asked me. When you've at last ensnared your duke, then can you have water fights and let your hair down and ride across meadows at crazy speeds?"

She opened her mouth and then closed it, having asked herself that very question just this week. Truth was, she didn't know if she could. She didn't know if she would be keeping herself perfectly and properly in check for the rest of her life.

"It looks as though we might not belong here as much as we thought, you and I."

Lucy immediately shook her head, a sort of fear he was correct washing through her. "That's not true. I do in fact belong here. My ancestry is royal, noble, and goes back for generations. I belong here as much as anyone. I've been poor, that's all, poor with excellent lineage. I've never lowered myself to…" She stopped. She was going to explain how they'd never worked as governesses, never been servants, though June had talked of doing just that right before Morley had stepped into their lives.

"Never lowered yourself? Never been a servant?" Mr. Sullivan's face closed off, and he bowed his head. "Beggin' your pardon, miss, I'll just see to your horses then." He turned from her.

"Wait, Mr. Sullivan. Will you still ride with me?"

He did not turn around but paused, his shoulders lowered, and then he nodded.

16

"What did you do to Mr. Sullivan?" Charity clucked, watching him walking away. "You know very well. I accidentally reminded him of our difference in station."

"Hm."

"Yes. It is for the best. What am I doing with Mr. Sullivan? Where could it possibly go?"

"At least now you're admitting that you're doing something with him." Charity's triumphant grin bothered Lucy.

"You needn't be so smug. Real lives are at stake here."

"I realize that. And of all the lives in our acquaintance, his is the most interesting." She shrugged. "But I'm not the one thinking about getting married."

"We have to get back and get ready for callers." Lucy did not wish to speak of him any longer. She hoped he'd leave London, and soon, so that she could move forward with her plans to be a duchess.

But one hour later, as their callers were taking tea, one second-year debutante, Constance, placed her cup in the saucer, her eyes full of excitement. "I almost forgot. Have you seen the new Mr. Sullivan?"

Lucy choked, suddenly overtaken by a fit of coughing brought on by the tea she had sucked into the back of her throat. "Goodness." She dabbed her lips. "What do you know of Mr. Sullivan?"

"He was promenading with Lord Fellon this morning. We were introduced, and he's asked me for the first set at Almacks."

Mr. Sullivan had been accepted into Almacks. "Extraordinary."

The woman sitting next to Constance nodded affirmatively. "I've heard he's the foremost expert on horses, that Prince George himself consults with the man, and that all doors are opened to him."

"And I've heard he's the most handsome man any of us has seen." The third giggled.

Lucy found herself wishing for them all to leave.

But Charity saved her and interrupted with news of the service and luncheon they could all attend to benefit the hungry children at the orphanages in London.

Lucy attempted to be distracted by her sister. In truth, she'd been more and more excited about her causes. But thoughts of Mr. Sullivan at Almacks outweighed every other thought.

She would be attending Almacks as well. That's all there was to it.

Then Lord Fellon arrived, and the ladies sat quietly, their eyes open, staring at him.

Lucy felt somewhat as though she were on stage, being scrutinized for her every syllable uttered.

And because she was playing a part.

Lord Fellon certainly felt it too for he stood to leave not long after he'd arrived.

When she walked toward the door at his side, he murmured, "There is to be a larger than usual crush at Almacks, will you be attending?"

"Uh—I, yes. I will."

"Excellent. Then my partner for the first and supper sets is intact." His grin made her laugh, briefly.

"I'll see you there."

He stepped out the door, his tall figure and thin frame an excellent match for her, she reminded herself. He was sensible. He was going to be a duke. And it's not as though the man wasn't handsome. His features were most certainly pleasing. He was everything Lucy had ever dreamed of marrying.

But all she could think about was how Mr. Sullivan was going to be at Almacks. Did the man know how to dance?

Then she remembered that indeed he did. They'd had a servants' ball in Brighton, for many of the local estates. And Lucy had volunteered to assist in putting it together. Mr. Sullivan danced well indeed.

She schooled her features as she reentered the drawing room, but her insides were a continued upheaval of emotion.

The remaining time for calling hours passed quickly. Lucy hardly heard as Charity managed most of the conversation and likely gave every woman present an education on the needed changes in their world.

When everyone had finally left, Charity leapt to her feet. "And now we must prepare for the meeting. Our service for the orphanages could start a regular tradition, and that could only be a good thing for these children long after we have blissfully returned to Brighton."

And then the footman announced, "A Lord Lockhart to see you, Miss Charity."

Lucy and Charity stood. Lucy was amazed for a moment to see her sister fidget. Her hands went to her front then her back and then at her side. Her face went blank and then filled with a smile.

"Hello, Miss Lucy, Miss Charity." He bowed. "Am I the only one here? We are feeding the children in the orphanages today, aren't we?"

"Oh. Oh yes, certainly. I believe you are the first to arrive, but that's wonderful. Shall we check on the cook in the kitchen and see what we can do to assist in preparing the kits?"

"Lead the way, fair maiden."

Charity snorted and then covered her mouth. "Lucy, could you see that the servants direct all newcomers to the kitchen?"

"Yes, I will."

At first, Lucy thought she would go nap in her room. Tonight was a dinner that might prove tiresome, and already the day had been rather full. But before she could step onto the first step going upstairs, she paused. And she knew she should help Charity. Her hand rested on the rail to go up. But she didn't move.

Then a knock on the door sounded behind her.

With a whirl of movement, the Duchess of York stepped into the front hall.

Lucy curtseyed. "Your Grace. How lovely of you to call."

"Yes, thank you. I'm here to assist Miss Charity and the orphans."

"Ah, excellent. I was just on my way to them. We are meeting in the kitchens to help assemble the kits, and then we will see that they are delivered."

"I should like to be there when they are delivered as well." Lucy led her through the main rooms of the house and then down to the back of the home where the kitchen was located.

Voices sounded. Whoever was working in the kitchen was having a jovial time of it, at least.

When Lucy and her grace entered the room, Lord Lockhart and Charity were assisting the kitchen staff and adding items to boxes in a line, each person standing in a row, adding one item at a time.

"Your Grace." Charity dipped a quick curtsey. Everyone else in the kitchen followed suit, including a respectful bow from Lord Lockhart.

Her grace jumped right in, loading bags of flour in the boxes.

They were joined by several others, and the efficiency picked up enough that they were soon prepared to make their deliveries.

Many of the women wanted to participate in the deliveries, enough that the Duchess of York called for her carriage again. Between the two, all the packages and the people were brought to the front doors of the orphanage in a working district of London.

The air smelt stale but not rancid. The warehouses and other businesses lined each street. The alleys leading off the main road seemed seedy and dark. Lucy would not wish to be traversing on any of those. But when the door opened, she was pleased to see that the inside of the building looked clean and orderly. It smelled nice, of the early hints of coming supper. Two women met them at the front door, one tall, the other short. Both with the lines of age and work making them interesting.

The duchess stepped forward. "Hello, I'd like to see that these donations reach the children."

"Oh, certainly." The taller woman moved to stand at her side. "I'm Adelaide Jones and the director of our home here. This food and these supplies will be in the children's hands today or on the shelves for later."

"Good to meet you, Miss Adelaide Jones. I am the Duchess of York."

The woman's face drained of color, and she fell to her knees in a deep curtsey from which she did not rise for many moments. When she finally did, she stood in silence.

Charity put an arm across her shoulders. "Miss Jones, where would you like us to leave these supplies?"

She seemed to snap out of her duchess-induced stupor and began to function.

Lucy laughed to herself. And then the air left her lungs. She might someday soon be like this duchess here, inspiring fear and happiness in those around her.

That thought was simply too foreign to contemplate while delivering boxes of food and supplies to the orphans.

People moved all around Lucy. She picked up a box and followed the others to a room with a long table.

Charity was more than pleased with the results of her organization. Lucy had not been aware of any of it, really, except vaguely that it was happening.

A young girl stepped up to Lucy and tugged on her dress. "Excuse me, miss."

"Yes?" Lucy dropped down to crouch in front of her.

The girl's wide eyes opened wider, and she swallowed. "Did you bring us any toys?"

Lucy looked to Charity, but her sister was busy talking with Adelaide about the logistics of putting everything where it needed to go. So Lucy smiled at the young girl. "I don't really know, but if I find out there's no toy, I'll send one back to you, how does that sound?"

The girl's eyes grew wider still, and she nodded.

"What is your name?"

"Julia." Her small voice found a place in Lucy's heart to nest.

"Thank you, Julia. I'll find out for you."

She nodded and stepped away, but then she turned back and wrapped her arms around Lucy's legs. With one tight squeeze, she sent a wave of happiness through Lucy and then ran off into another room.

Tears sprung to Lucy's eyes, and when her gaze caught Charity's, they shared a moment of such happiness that Lucy wanted to do much more of this. She nodded at her sister, so proud to be a part of something important.

They distributed and sorted and organized all the donations for the orphanage and then were back on their way to the Duchess of Sussex's home.

As soon as they walked in the door, her grace called them into the front room. "As you know, we have been included in a dinner this evening, hosted by the Duke of Kent, and I've just received word that Prince George himself will attend, with his new horse expert. Apparently, he's a genius in training and purchasing, and the men are all competing for a moment of his time." She fanned herself. "This is good news as well as bad. For I don't think Lord Fellon has been invited. What good can come of being so closely connected to the prince with no one to see it? But good news because it is an excellent connection, and I think that with or without Lord Fellon, you are well on your way to being one of the most well-connected debutantes of the season."

"Thank you, Your Grace. And what is the bad news?"

"The bad?" She waved a hand. "Oh, it's Prinny. He's unpredictable at best and might attempt a wildly inappropriate flirtation."

Lucy nodded, trying to take in all the new information.

"But the best news is that your dresses from the modiste have arrived, and you may choose one to wear."

She tried to respond with appropriate excitement about the new dresses, but all that really made an impact in her mind was the added bit of information most people probably overlooked. The prince would bring his stablemaster. Mr. Sullivan.

17

The Duke of Kent was the largest man Lucy had ever seen. He looked as tall as he was broad. And his furniture was all made to fit him. As it was, Lucy felt like a small child, sitting in an armchair in the front drawing room of his home.

Charity sat in the chair opposite but seemed very far indeed. The Duchess of Kent sat beside Charity and poured her tea. "Thank you for coming, my dear. Tonight shall be enlightening for the men, but I expect it to be so for the women as well." She smiled.

"I'm pleased to hear it and so honored to be included."

"The Duchess of Sussex has been a good friend for many years. It's a rather daunting task to become a duchess, a royal one at that. You will see when his highness arrives." She looked pained for a moment. "The royal family bring with them certain…qualities. And immense power."

The guest list seemed to be very privileged indeed. Every man in the room was a duke so far, and every woman their equivalent in rank or notoriety or wealth. Everyone except for Lucy and Charity.

Lucy swallowed, trying to think of what to say to answer her grace.

Then Charity placed her tea on the table in front of them. "I find the idea of a royal family fascinating. They can affect the culture of an entire country, their religion, their choice in food preference. They can impoverish or enrich a nation. And to live one's life in a situation where every need is met, every whim granted. With endless resources at your fingertips." She shook her head. "Can you imagine what good you could do? I for one hope to converse with the prince. Has anyone yet told him that women would like to have a vote?"

Lucy stiffened, but the Duchess of Kent merely laughed. "You won't get very far with him until you prove you can be jovial and entertaining." She shook her head. "Unfortunately."

"Perhaps we can spend the time learning and not...speaking." Lucy did not want this evening to involve Charity and her many engaging conversations with groups of men. What did she discuss with them? Lucy had never participated, just seen her from across rooms.

"Really, Miss Lucy. Your sister can converse about whatever she likes. You will find members of our dinner party to have surprising opinions themselves."

"Thank you, Your Grace." The look Charity gave Lucy tugged at her heart. She was obviously hurt.

And the more Lucy thought about Charity, her efforts, her heart, that little girl Julia came to mind, and Lucy wished to recant her nudge to silence Charity. The woman should be heard. Just perhaps not in a situation that might hurt Lucy's chances at marrying. She sighed. "I'm sorry, sister."

"I know."

Delicious smells wafted in their direction. The dinner promised to be a delectable affair if nothing else. And Lucy was determined to impress them or, at the very least, not embarrass herself.

How would Mr. Sullivan fare with such a group? He would likely need some assistance. Perhaps she would be able to ease his way somewhat in that group. She watched the door from her overly large chair. Every movement from that direction caught her eye.

But even as the time to move into the dining room with their group drew near, neither he nor the prince had arrived.

She and Charity stood to walk the room together. As they approached the Dukes of York and Sussex, Lucy was interested to see if the same rivalry existed between the two men.

The Duke of York downed his tea as if it were something stronger. "I will consult with the Sullivan fellow. I'm looking to increase my stables and the breeding we have just begun. I think we've acquired rights to a foal from Mandane. She was incredible on the track. Her sire was renowned Pot-8-Os."

Lucy linked arms with her sister. "Does our Mr. Sullivan know enough to help all these men?"

Charity clucked. "I don't think he is our Mr. Sullivan any longer. And I don't know. But he must know something of great value to be the prince's help at the Royal Pavilion stables. And to accompany him to a party such as this? I can only guess that his opinion is valuable indeed."

"It must be." They walked past the dukes and to the window overlooking the street. "Such a lovely situation."

The house sat on Grosvenor Square but backed to an expanse of green. Charity's words, "not our Mr. Sullivan any longer," repeated themselves in different ways as they bounced around in her mind. How could he not be their Mr.

Sullivan? Were they not friends? She thought of their shared experiences. In almost every one, he was their stable hand. Was he merely acting as her employee, or did they in fact have a friendship as she had always supposed? Did they have more? The dangerous thought tightened her grip on Charity. Her sister raised an eyebrow. "Are you nervous?"

"I am."

"I don't think you're nervous about the prince, so it must be his new protege?"

"Mr. Sullivan and I." She pressed her lips together, uncertain how to continue. "I'm not certain how to proceed."

"Perhaps let him lead the way on that. He might have his own expectations on how he would like to be treated."

"True. Perhaps I shall treat him like I would any gentleman?"

"Perhaps. Or perhaps he will seek more intimate conversation. I believe you can safely follow his lead."

"Charity, I am sorry that I even suggested you keep your thoughts to yourself. You are here in a room full of influential people. When else will you get this chance?"

"What about your...aspirations?"

"Lord Fellon isn't present. As long as your conversations don't get us talked about throughout the ton, I think we are safe to discuss whatever we would like."

Charity considered her. "I shall approach the subjects gently."

The Duchess of York joined them. "And now we must hear from you, Charity. You will prove to be the most interesting member of this party, without question."

The footman returned at the door.

"At long last, goodness, that man is inconsiderate." The duchess fanned herself.

The prince was announced, and everyone stood and then lowered into curtseys and bows. Then the footman announced, "Mr. Sullivan."

Lucy's gaze snapped to his.

His eyes were on her. With a small smile, he nodded then dipped his head again to everyone in the room.

"My, he's handsome." Charity's murmured, uncharacteristic assessment sounded a mite too breathy in Lucy's mind, but when she turned to her sister, the humor on her face told her that Lucy was being teased.

"Oh, would you stop."

"I'm sorry, but what can I do? This is the stuff of books and fairy tales."

The Duchess of York watched the two of them too closely, so Lucy waved her fingers. "If only Lord Fellon were here."

"Is Lord Fellon interested in horses as well?" Her grace closed her fan and tapped it against her palm.

"He is. I saw him with Mr. Sullivan at the park this week."

"Oh, so are you acquainted with Mr. Sullivan already then?"

"We are. Yes. He seems very knowledgeable."

"That's not all he seems." Her grace's wink sent Lucy's eyes back to Mr. Sullivan.

He was more handsome every time she saw him. His cravat was more elaborately tied. His shoulders filled out the cut of his jacket. His jawline was strong, sharp. She could hardly keep from looking at him, trying to see where the stable hand she knew and this new paragon fit together. "No, it's not."

The older woman laughed. "Come now, Miss Lucy. By all appearances, he would be an excellent catch." She indicated a group of men, some of the more powerful dukes in England, gathered around her old servant.

"Uncanny." She could not make sense of what she was seeing.

Then the prince approached. They curtseyed low again, and he kissed each of their hands. "I hear we have some cousins in the Molyneaux line with us this evening." He stood taller than them both, his clothing all but stretched across his middle, his face, his jawline, drooping, his cravat crisp. He was certainly elaborately dressed but, in a surprising manner, also understated.

"Are we cousins?" Charity rose from her curtsey.

"In a manner of speaking. Distant relations, perhaps? I've often heard of the Standish Sisters of Sussex and their plight and then their remarkable return to comfort. The castle is looking almost better than its purported original splendor. Lord Morley is to be congratulated."

"Thank you. We feel blessed and happy indeed."

"Perhaps this sort of thing is precisely what old Molyneaux desired for his descendants. You can never prepare too much for the generations that come."

The duchess huffed to herself. "Indeed."

"And how are you, sister?"

"Your brother has updated you no doubt on the children?"

"He did not."

"We are well. Charles returns from Eton any day for his break."

"Ah, very good. He must come and show me a thing or two about cricket, no doubt."

"I'll pass along the invitation."

While the two in-laws discussed family matters, Lucy turned her attention once again to Mr. Sullivan. The Duke of

Sussex guffawed in large laughter and clapped Mr. Sullivan on the back.

He seemed relaxed and comfortable in his new company. A footman arrived again at the door. "Dinner is served." The prince offered his arm to the Duchess of Kent. The duke then offered his arm to Charity, with a nod at Lucy.

Charity placed a hand on his arm, his girth keeping her a further distance from himself. But something she said immediately sent him to laughter. And Lucy was amazed again at her sister's ability to engage the men of the ton in conversation. She should not discount her so often. Charity was gifted with words, as was so often apparent. Even the duchesses were showing an interest in her causes.

The room paired off, and Lucy began to see the predictive writing on the wall. As she turned to Mr. Sullivan, he approached from across the room.

At last, when there was only he and she, he extended his arm. "Might I escort you in to dinner, Miss Lucy?"

She placed her hand on his arm. "Thank you."

They entered. Charity was seated by the Duke of Kent, surrounded by the others. Mr. Sullivan was to be seated by the prince, but His Highness lifted a hand. Everyone went quiet. "Move Mr. Sullivan down by a pretty lady at least. He doesn't need to be talking horses for all of dinner."

The servants immediately made the changes, and before she knew it, she and Mr. Sullivan were sitting together at the end of the table by the Duchess of Kent.

"Well, isn't this more cozy for you, Mr. Sullivan?" Their hostess smiled, looking from one to the other.

He nodded, looking pleased himself, and the charm of his white teeth, the sparkle in his eyes, made her wish to clench something. He was rather handsome. More so up close. How did every woman in the room not swoon in his presence?

"I'm pleased as can be to be seated in this place of honor."

"Well, and we are happy to have you. The prince has taken quite a liking."

"He's been good to my father and me. Our stables will now rise considerably with his support and attention."

"Well deserved. He is good to see talent where it lies." Lucy felt the need to acknowledge it would not be simply the prince's recommendation that made his fame.

"Thank you, Miss Lucy. Loyalty from a friend is valuable indeed."

"Are the two of you acquainted well then?" Her grace looked from one to the other with new eyes.

"We are friends from home, in Brighton." Lucy smiled.

"Lucy's horses are some of the first to benefit from the Sullivan care." His grin, hiding all their secrets, made Lucy wish to laugh.

"And my Firestone might love him more than she does me, though I daren't admit such a thing often."

"A more loyal horse you could not find."

She looked forward to their ride more than ever.

A line of footmen brought in the first course. While her grace engaged Mr. Sullivan in conversations, Lucy sipped her soup and listened to the talk around them.

"Mr. Sullivan. Has Miss Lucy made introductions for you? With the prince, surely you will meet every noble in London with a slight interest in horses, but the ladies. You must also meet the ladies. You are quite the catch, you know." Her grace smiled and winked at Miss Lucy.

A second duchess now telling Lucy that her stable hand was quite the catch. While confusion swirled ever more, she stumbled over her next words. "We have not, that is, no. I shall need to do just that. Thank you, Your Grace."

Mr. Sullivan rested a hand on her forearm for the briefest moment, his smile apologetic even, but the fleeting touch sent a rush of awareness that caught her unprepared. Her face flushed, and she had to concentrate to use a steady hand to take her next sip of water.

"She has been more than generous to her old friend. This is the first invitation to which we've both been invited."

"Ah, we shall have to rectify that at any rate. With a woman friend at your side, many more introductions are available."

Lucy's discomfort grew. Would he be trying to woo the other ladies of the ton? Not for the first time, she was astounded at the world flipped upside down that brought her forbidden secret interest to her side in the midst of the ton. She could not be grateful yet for such a boon as he had come on the cusp of a rising relationship with Lord Fellon, the situation she had long desired.

A sudden desire to stand and walk in brisk air could not be honored. Instead, the servants brought the next course.

When the duchess seemed well and truly distracted, Mr. Sullivan leaned closer. "This must be trying for you."

She dared a look into his face. His eyes were close, caring, interested. He could never hide his interest, not completely, though perhaps he was just always polite, kind, interested because she was his employer?

The confusion increased, warring with her peace.

"I confess I do not know what to think."

"Perhaps we can talk unrestrained on our ride?"

She nodded. "I'd like that."

He lifted his cup. "In the meantime, this game of pretend

is quite delicious." He took a sip, his gaze travelling over her face, leaving a path of warmth. Pretend? She was well and truly feeling the reality of him at her side.

But she played along, daring herself along the way. Her next bite entered her mouth slowly. She thrilled that she had his full attention. "Perhaps it is more delicious than I thought, fun even?"

"Like letting your hair down." His eyes danced with amusement, knowing this tidbit about her.

"Hm. Quite. You did suggest I do that if I enjoy it so."

"And this might be enjoyable too?" He lifted his cup to hers.

As she studied his face, she knew that it would be, dangerously and deliciously enjoyable. "Yes, it shall."

His slow smile grew and sent a wave of happy gooseflesh through her. No man deserved to be so handsome. Then they each drank on their silent pact.

"Shall I come calling tomorrow for our ride?"

"Yes, I'd like that. We can go together to the stables."

"And then perhaps ices?"

"Do you think they're anything close to the ices in Brighton?"

"We shall have to taste them to know for certain."

"Then ices it is."

"And perhaps a promenade?"

She opened her mouth, ready to laugh at his growing list, but saw that he was completely earnest.

"How badly do you want to let your hair down?"

"Perhaps we shall take it one pin at a time then?"

He nodded. "One pin at a time."

18

Lucy waited at the front door for Mr. Sullivan to arrive. The footman stood at the ready to open the door. And Lucy refused to feel ridiculous.

Charity walked out with a book in hand and stopped. "What are you doing?"

"Oh, I'm ready for my ride this morning."

"You certainly are." Her grin grew, but she said nothing more and continued round the corner.

Lucy was ridiculous and she knew it, but this new opportunity, the daring behavior of their plan, filled her with such a compelling urgent need she didn't know what else to do. She must see Mr. Sullivan today. And she must see him as soon as possible. She could no sooner change those demands than change the course of the Thames.

And so she waited.

And he was late.

But when the knocker finally sounded, she flung the door open herself. "Mr. Sullivan!"

His eyes widened. "Miss Lucy."

She called over her shoulder, "We shall be off." Then she placed a hand on his arm as he led her back down the front stoop and down the drive.

"Do either of us know how to get to the stables?"

She stopped and then laughed. "I think they are in that direction." She pointed left.

"Then left we shall go."

She paused. The duchess's butler opened the door. "Miss?"

"Could you direct us in the location of the stables? I'd like to visit my horse."

"Certainly. If you follow that lane, there is a lovely walk in front of estates and larger homes, and at the end of the lane sits the stables."

"Sounds wonderful."

They started down the lane, and she felt as old friends do. "Is it odd that I feel so comfortable around you?"

"Why would it be?"

"We've never really behaved as chums before."

"And are we…chums?"

She laughed. "Well, no. Hardly," she breathed, not daring express much further. But she could no sooner think of Mr. Sullivan as a chum as she could view the sky red. It was beyond those limitations. Far beyond.

"We have spent many an hour together. I do not find it too strange that there is a level of comfort." He placed a hand on hers. "And you've let your hair down so to speak."

She laughed, remembered their challenge from earlier. "Pin by pin." She shook her head. "I don't know if you're good for me, Mr. Sullivan."

"I have some thoughts about that very thing."

"Do you?"

"Yes, I do."

"This I'd like to hear."

"And you shall. We are to have an unrestrained conversation, am I right?"

She thrilled and feared at the same time what might be said. And she reminded herself that in all this bravado and flirtation, she had best mind her tongue.

But she couldn't resist him, not really, not on such a beautiful day. "Mr. Sullivan, I suspect that this one outing might be my most enjoyable time so far in London."

"Yes, I can well imagine, having participated in some of these events of the ton. And Firestone is hard to beat."

She laughed. "Have you not enjoyed yourself?"

"I have, certainly. But after one or two dinners, they are all the same."

"Most people would not consider a dinner with the royal dukes and the prince himself to be mundane."

"Truly, you are most correct. And I don't imagine most dinners include an inebriate prince dancing his own reel down the middle of the floor."

"Certainly not." Lucy laughed, remembering the prince during the later of the dinner hours. "And I admit to being grateful that his antics ended that evening."

"I as well, particularly knowing that I would be seeing you this very next day."

"We can thank him for putting us close together."

"I already have."

"What? You did? What did he say? What did you say?"

"I said, merely the truth, that you are the closest friend I have in this town. And that if I behaved in just the right way, perhaps I might convince you that I am no longer merely your stable hand." He didn't look at her when he said it. And by the way he carried himself, carefully, purposefully, she knew that his statement was much more than a whim or a flirt.

"And did he think you would find success?"

"He did, in a manner of speaking."

"Which was?"

"He said that I was quite a catch, and when he was done with me, I'd be sinfully wealthy besides." He laughed. "Which sounds beyond my dreams wonderful. And he said that if you weren't able to overlook our past relationship, others would." He winced. "Perhaps I shouldn't have repeated that part."

"Well, I'm not surprised as two of the royal duchesses last night told me how much of a catch you are."

They walked in silence for a moment more. "But their predictions matter very little to me."

She nodded.

"There is only one I care to know."

And then her alarm bells sounded. She had Lord Fellon. She had her goals. She had her dreams, her family to think of.

But before she could think of a way to diffuse the intensity, he reached for her hand. "But I'm more excited to get up on a horse than this stately walk will allow." He gave her hand a little tug. "Shall we pick up our pace?"

At first, she was inclined to deny her sudden urge to follow, but then his daring expression, the laugh on his lips were too much to resist, and she lifted her skirts with one hand and allowed herself to fly over the dirt beneath her feet with Mr. Sullivan at her side.

They ran in between estate homes, on paths lined with thick stone walls. Climbing roses hung over the tops, archways of leaves from tall trees swept overhead, and the sweet smell of flowers filled the air. The air was crisp and clean, the sky blue, the sun just warm enough, and Mr. Sullivan's hand in her own held promises. The suggestion of many days ahead just as wonderful.

She could hardly resist the joy of it all.

When they arrived at the stable gate, she took a moment to catch her breath.

"You've lost one already." Mr. Sullivan held up a hairpin.

"What? Have I?" She laughed, but the significance was not lost on her. "I have rarely had so much enjoyment in the losing of a hairpin."

"Nor I." He laughed. "Though I confess to never having lost one."

"You." She smiled. "Come on. I long to see my horse."

They approached, and a stable hand came forward. "What can I do for you, miss?"

Mr. Sullivan shook his head. "We'll take care of things from here."

When the stable hand looked ready to complain, Lucy shook her head. "I'm Miss Lucy, Firestone is my mare, and this is the Mr. Sullivan. We are in the presence of a horse expert."

"Ah yes, very good, miss." His eyes widened as he looked Mr. Sullivan over. But her escort didn't seem to notice.

He breathed deeply and stretched his neck against his cravat. "Now, this feels more like home."

"I agree with you there." She followed him in. "I don't know where they've placed Firestone."

Her familiar whinny sounded, and Mr. Sullivan led the way. "She's right this way. I've had her placed in the larger stalls and given an extra feeding of oats."

"What? You've come to see to my horse?"

"Certainly." He dipped his head. "It's my job, miss."

But when she felt a bit at odds with that statement, he added, "I couldn't let Firestone stay in a strange place with no familiar faces about her. And who knows if they'd give her the rubdown she was used to."

Lucy stood closer. "Thank you."

"You're most welcome." He glanced down at her twice before adding, "and I knew you'd wish it were so."

His concern, his awareness of her single most important possession, his care, she had to admit she was shaken by the depth of her gratitude and her heart-pounding, breath-halting reaction to him. There was no question he knew how to reach her. Lord Fellon hardly knew of her interest in horses.

To be fair, he'd never served as her stable hand.

But also, to be fair, he'd likely never ask about her horse or listen to a response.

Was it cruel to be shown a man so suitable in personality while so opposite of what she'd always thought she needed?

Cruel or provident?

His ready smile approached Firestone, and even though the handsome expression was directed at her horse, Lucy felt the power of it, of his presence. And she could only hope that life held no cruel twists of fate.

"Hey, girl." Firestone snorted and pushed her nose up over the gate to her stall. She hugged her horse, breathing in the smell of her, appreciating her shiny coat. "She is well cared for indeed."

Mr. Sullivan watched her, and when she turned grateful eyes in his direction, he nodded. "As if she were my own."

"Thank you. I don't even know what we will do without you in Brighton." She sighed. "This is all so complicated, isn't it?"

"I don't see how it has to be." He stepped toward the

storage room. "I'll get the saddles. Which horse do you think I should ride?"

"Do you know these horses?"

"A bit. Do you think the duke would have thoughts about someone riding his stallion?"

"Oh yes, I'm sure he would."

"Then I'll be riding that pretty mare over there." He indicated a gray speckled horse with a dark brown mane.

"She is stunning. What a beautiful animal." She left Firestone for a moment to greet the new horse. The sign above her stall read, "Cloud." She nuzzled into Lucy's hand. "She's a love, this one."

"I'm hoping she can keep up with our Firestone. You might need to take it easy on us."

"Sadly, there's nowhere we can ride that will even test Firestone's abilities. This will be slow and staid. No cliffs of Brighton here."

"Well now, that doesn't sound like the Miss Lucy I know."

"Well now, you might just have to trust my knowledge of how we do things here in London."

"How you do things? Or how they do things?"

Confusion warred inside, and a new irritation rose at the limits he was attempting to push.

But he held up his hands. "Stop right there. I see I have overstepped."

"You forget."

"No. Unfortunately, I always remember." His eyes held sadness. But then he handed her the saddle. "Miss?"

Her eyebrow rose in challenge. "Very well." She took the saddle and lifted it and the blanket up onto Firestone. Then she adjusted everything, tightened the straps, and went in search of a bridle.

But he met her at the stall gate, holding one for her.

"Thank you."

"I love it that you can saddle your own horse."

She knew her cheeks burned brightly, but she just turned away. "As you should. Turns out I had the best teacher in all of the ton, sponsored by the prince himself."

"Does the prince's support change my abilities?"

"Not at all. You've always been magnificent. Your father and you run the best stables anyone has ever seen."

He laughed to himself. "But the prince's support does change things."

She considered him. "Yes, it does."

"For you?"

That was a question she could not easily answer. So she didn't.

And he didn't ask again.

When it was time to ride, he stepped up behind her, close, so that when she turned to find him, he was there and ready.

The hands he placed on her hips felt familiar. The smell that filled the air around them was welcoming. She placed hands on his shoulders that seemed to know the way there. And when she searched his eyes, it was with a longing to stay, very near, for a very long time.

Did he share her longing? He might, but he kept it hidden. His strong hands had her up on her horse and adjusting her skirts without even a seeming strain on his part.

His hand at her stirrup, wrapped around her ankle, did not feel at all familiar. But she thrilled at his touch. He gave her a gentle squeeze. "You look good up there, Miss Lucy."

"Thank you, Mr. Sullivan."

He leapt up on Cloud, and they left the stables side by side out into the sunlight.

And everything was right in the world.

And then it was wrong.

Lord Fellon approached from the distance.

She groaned.

"Is that?"

"Yes."

"Should we hide?"

"Surely he can see us."

"I don't think he can, not enough to identify us. Come on, this way." He tore down a side lane. And so without looking again at the small rider and horse that was Lord Fellon approaching, she followed.

"What are you doing?"

"I'm having a ride in the park with you no matter what."

"That's the thing about London. People are never alone here. The park will be full of people."

"But not your almost intended."

That was true. But still, did she feel comfortable running away from the first sight of Lord Fellon? Did she not wish to marry the man?

She did. She thought. But could she not have this little diversion first? Could she not explore how much she needed to feel attraction and caring for the man she married? Because the feelings she had for Lord Fellon and Mr. Sullivan were different indeed.

They raced along, picking up speed as they realized the length of the lane.

"We need to turn off somewhere." Lucy strived to ride higher to see over a wall. She was too short.

"There's a hedgerow up ahead."

"Which likely leads to someone's estate."

"We won't stay on it long."

She groaned inside. She had a reputation to uphold. His might come and go. His was of such that he was protected in a sense as a man and as a friend to the prince and as someone who had valuable information.

Hers was as fragile as her tentative relationship with Lord Fellon.

But as Mr. Sullivan picked up speed, she followed and a laugh built up in her throat and bubbled over. "I can't believe we're doing this."

He turned down a small path and then leapt over a gate.

She followed suit, Firestone as eager for adventure as she was apparently. They raced up a small path in single file until it reached another wider lane. This area seemed less populated. And in fact, Lucy suspected it was one of the roads that led out of town to the country estates that cinched up against London on the west. Firestone moved to walk beside Cloud, and Lucy had to laugh at the self-satisfied grin on Mr. Sullivan's face.

"What is this?"

"This?" He turned all of the power of his smile on her. "This is the joy a man feels when he knows he has an uninterrupted afternoon with a beautiful woman."

She sucked in her breath. "Mr. Sullivan."

He shook his head. "No. I cannot resist. I cannot pretend I don't feel. We are on horses, riding out into the countryside, and I'm as pleased as Mama's pie about it."

She laughed at that, finally seeing more of the Mr. Sullivan that she had known these many months. "Well, I'm pleased as Mama's pie about it too."

"Are you?" He searched her face.

"I am."

He nodded. "Just so."

They rode for a minute more, and then he started talking about his new position with the prince, about his business, about the different parts of England where it might be nice to purchase land. He talked about his father and how the man was just as happy working the stables as he was owning a single thing.

"My father has real pride in the castle and the land about. He knows his father and his father before him have cared for the horses there. The bloodlines are some of the best in England. I don't think Morley even knows some of the stock you have in those horses."

"That's wonderful. We have no end of respect for your family, you must know."

"Yes, you've been the finest employers and dear friends besides."

"Friends."

"Yes. There was a time I didn't even dare claim friendship, but I think I can safely do so now, at least that?" The hope in his gaze, the pretended indifference when she knew he was preparing to be hurt, shot straight to her heart.

"Yes, I think we had decided long ago that our families are friends."

"True. You had, hadn't you?"

"And perhaps distant cousins as well."

He turned away. "I don't know if it matters, discovering that your family might have blended with a commoner and was banished from the family tree is disheartening. Kind of humbling for a stable hand to hear."

"But wonderful to know you have that other family line in there as well. I mean, I assume it might be wonderful. We have found the discovery of that knowledge and how we all fit together to be enlightening."

"Because everything you've discovered about your family so far has been uplifting and has risen you in station."

"And you don't seem to be suffering from any demotions in station since discovering your heritage."

"That's true, but you know it's unrelated."

"Might not be. Royals have a distinct ability to remember who is royal and who isn't. I wouldn't be surprised if there's some knowledge of the whole story in some royal book somewhere."

He laughed for a minute. "Do they really care that much?"

"Yes. Royals really care about their lineage."

"I suppose the whole ton cares. It's all about heirs and family and nobility, isn't it?"

"Yes, it is." Thinking of all the time she'd spent caring about just such a thing, she said no more for a minute.

"And you're right there with them. You care about things like rank and title too."

And here was the opportunity for them to start their very frank discussion, and she was loathe to do so. But she knew it would help in the long run for him to know where she stood. "And for good reason. If I can marry a duke's son, my children and their children and all the children of even my sisters for generations will be taken care of."

He was quiet for a time, his horse ambling along with Firestone at his side. "And money wouldn't be enough?"

"I don't know. It's enough, but a duke usually has the type of estates, multiple, that can provide and continue to provide for families for generations. And the title alone affords the family certain privileges."

"Don't you already have all those privileges? Don't you claim royal connections?"

"Distantly, yes, and it wasn't enough." She gasped. "It

really was the money that mattered in our situation. We had none, and those with the responsibility to care for us didn't leave us any. And all the titles in the world did nothing. " Her world shifted. With the handsome Mr. Sullivan riding beside her and the realization that even a dukedom didn't guarantee anything, she wondered once again if everything she'd always wanted was not exactly what she wanted anymore.

19

Their ride was by far the most enjoyable time she'd had in London. But as they led the horses into the stables, the magic of just being together and pretending everything would be all right started to fade. They put the saddles away and took off the bridles in silence. She picked up a brush from the stable buckets and started to brush down Firestone. Mr. Sullivan stepped into Firestone's stall with her and lifted a hand to her brush, resting his fingers over the top of hers. His were strong, slightly callused, large. And the feel of his skin on hers felt warm. They moved the brush together down Firestone's back and then up to her neck, going down her back again. Over and over, they ran the brush along her coat. Her body hummed with desire. He was so close behind her; the air between them drew her closer. She closed her eyes, filled with the smells of the stables, of Firestone, and of Mr. Sullivan. His earthy, bold scent smelled like home. The feel of Mr. Sullivan's body behind her, his strong arms around her, his hand over hers as they moved the brush were almost too much for her. Her breath came faster, and her mouth went completely dry. It was all she could do to just keep brushing, because if she stopped, what would happen next?

He put his other hand on her shoulder. "Lucy."

She swallowed and then looked down.

"Turn around."

She didn't even try to stop herself. When she faced him, they were close, not as close as she'd imagined, but she could put her hand on his chest, or his arm, or even up around the back of his neck if she liked. "You called me Lucy."

"It just came out. I apologize. Miss Lucy." His voice was soft, but it rumbled through her like a storm, shaking her up, sending sparks of light in random places. She didn't think she would ever be the same.

He stepped closer, and she leaned back against Firestone. The horse's warm flank, the feel of her heart at Lucy's back, made her bold, gave her strength.

Mr. Sullivan lifted a hand and rested it on Firestone just above Lucy's shoulder. "Thank you for our ride today."

She lifted her lashes to stare into caring eyes, and suddenly she knew Mr. Sullivan was not going to try and kiss her. But he wanted to. His gaze dropped to her mouth, lingered there for what felt like a long time, and then the sparkling happiness in his eyes found hers again.

He was about to step away, but she reached a hand out to his arm. "Wait. When will I see you again?"

"I come here often."

"Will you be at any balls? Or events or things?"

"I never know. I'm at the mercy of whoever might extend an invitation. I could come calling."

She considered him and then nodded. "I'd love to see you."

"If you need to reach me, the help here, they know where

to find me." He drank in her face, as if he'd never see her again, and then he stepped away. "I'll see you soon."

She nodded.

"Oh, and the hands, they can bring you home in a cart if you like."

"Where are you going?"

"I forgot I have an appointment." He kept walking.

"With who?"

"If you must know, with Lord Fellon." The awkwardness of that statement settled over them both.

"Hm. We're going to a reading tonight. Will you be there?"

"I don't think so."

She watched him until he rounded the corner. And then she slumped back against the wall to the stables. What on earth was she going to do now?

She closed the gate to Firestone's stall. A stable hand agreed to take her back to the house in a donkey cart. And before long, she was in her room taking a bath.

Hours later, she wore one of her new dresses with Charity at her side, and the two attended a reading at the home of Lord Bailey. Lucy didn't know him well at all, but from what she could tell of the man who never seemed pleased, he enjoyed expressing his displeasure to all those around him. They made their way into the larger drawing room which was set with many chairs from around their home. Lucy was charmed by the different sizes and shapes of the chairs. Some were obviously from the dining room, some from a sitting room, some quite possibly from the schoolroom.

She and Charity took their places toward the back. "This will prove to be very interesting. I am most intrigued by the selections."

Lucy was feeling dissatisfied. "I suppose we must save this place for Lord Fellon."

"You suppose?" Charity's one eyebrow rose, characteristically higher than usual.

And Lucy laughed. "My dear sister. Yes, we must save him a spot." She sighed.

"But you don't want to." Her searching expression made Lucy wish she'd said nothing at all.

"I want to. Of course I do. But what will my brain think when you on one side are thinking all the most animated of thoughts and he on the other the most dull and lifeless possible?"

Charity studied her for many minutes. "If he is so dull and lifeless…"

"He is not. He merely pretends to be. Have you not noticed the way of the ton? They all act as though life is boring. For to be animated, to be truly moved by something is juvenile. And they aren't as learned as they would like. They are to only briefly touch on the subjects, not to delve, not to impassion."

"And all my passion?"

"It is an oddity for them but an embraced one. I've never seen the men flock to a woman with ideas before." Lucy laughed. "Perhaps I shall attempt an idea."

"I highly recommend thinking for oneself and voicing said thoughts."

"Well, perhaps if we could all be as beautiful as you…" She studied her sister's red hair, thick and beautiful.

"As if your blond tresses and soft blue eyes are not the epitome of ton perfection, Lucy."

"Well, how do you manage it then?"

"I manage to engage their curiosity, not their amorous

declarations of love." A glimmer of pain flickered across her face. "But I would not lower myself to please them. I will not speak of dull things. And I will always challenge their views. If there is not a man who can admire such a woman, then there is not a man for me." Something in her face led Lucy to believe perhaps Charity had hopes for a certain man. But now was not the time to be delving into the particulars.

"I shall attempt to engage him in conversation. Real thoughts, my real feelings." She filled her chest with air, the trepidation for the task she was about to complete rising. How could it be so difficult to merely express one's true thoughts?

She closed her eyes, facing the reality she'd always known. Because she didn't believe she truly met all the requirements to be a duchess. She didn't naturally fill the role. But she had learned to train herself to be. And she could pretend. Forever if she needed to. But what if, what if there was some way to blend the two? What if she could be herself and a duchess at the same time?

The ride today with Mr. Sullivan had been so freeing. She'd felt comfortable and, at the same time, energized. She wished to be herself and more than herself. And everything else from that moment until this had felt strangely lackluster, without purpose, and absolutely foreign to her true nature.

And those were dangerous thoughts, indeed, thoughts that led her away from her dream, away from happiness with Lord Fellon. As she felt the nudges of freedom beckoning to her, she longed to regain the satisfaction she'd felt in her earlier plan. Who did not wish to be a duchess?

When Lord Fellon at last arrived, he entered with three other lords, men Lucy did not particularly enjoy. They moved together toward the front when one caught sight of her and indicated her location to Lord Fellon.

Did he seem disappointed when he turned from them to come take his spot beside her? He might have.

She sat taller. She could rally. They could broaden their relationship and share more of their true selves. And she held her breath, hoping she would still be acceptable to him when she did so.

His smile was natural, and he moved his chair to be closer to her. When he reached for her hand, she was pleased, though there was nothing exciting about the gesture, no reaction inside begging for more, none of the amazing attraction she felt when she was with Mr. Sullivan.

But that was to be expected.

Or so she told herself. She and Lord Fellon were not a love match.

Did that mean that she and Mr. Sullivan would be? Her heart raced in rebellion. And she tried desperately to push that line of thinking aside.

Lord Fellon squeezed her hand in his, a gentle gesture, almost like a greeting, and then he smiled. "How have you been?"

"Excellent. I've made some new acquaintances."

"I heard you were at the Kent dinner with the prince."

"Yes, it was enlightening as well as providential for me to make such elevated acquaintances."

"I'm pleased they all seem as accepting of you as I am. You are the diamond that I saw in you when we met." His smile was genuine, and she should have exulted in such high praise, but she could hardly believe it or count it as valuable. She was successful. Society was accepting her. But did he? Did Lord Fellon enjoy her company? Did he even like her?

"I've been so focused on my horses, but it has been fascinating to learn how I can make our stock better. I've enjoyed our new Mr. Sullivan and all of his insight. I've made a huge purchase at Tattersall's that he has advised might double our value in less than a decade."

"That's wonderful. He seems a valuable asset indeed."

"Yes, he is. When he gains his own establishment, he will be the only competition for our stables. He and perhaps the prince who he is managing right now."

"Oh?"

"Certainly. But his acceptance in our circles can be as short lived as we need it to be." His grin turned cunning, and Lucy wondered just what he was planning to do.

"I'm not privy to these ways, but once he is a landed gentleman, he will always have that status, will he not?"

"Certainly. But you and I have seen the rise and fall of people's reputations. At times, a reputation can be as fragile as glass."

She nodded, willing her hands to remain still.

"You sisters have always maintained the best of reputations even in your more difficult times. It is those kinds of long-held traditions that speak of the truly good families in our midst. The trusted worthy bloodlines will always speak truth through the generations."

Lucy's concern rose higher. Trusted worthy bloodlines. Had she not said similar things in the past? Had she not spoken of the surety of the dukedom for her family?

"I am grateful we have found each other. I hope I might speak to someone on your behalf?" He leaned closer. His expression was sincere.

She nodded slowly. "Yes, Lord Morley is considered a guardian of sorts and handles conversations for us."

Charity stiffened beside Lucy, and she knew she could

have phrased that differently. But tosh. This was the moment she'd been waiting for. He would speak of marriage?

"And I'd love to request a private moment alone with you this week, if I may?"

"I look forward to it." She smiled, her most demure, appreciative smile. And told herself perhaps now was not the moment to begin discussing things outside their normal range of conversation.

Their host stood up at the front of the room, ready to introduce the remaining program for the evening.

20

T he final reading of the evening proved to be interesting indeed. Charity squeezed Lucy's arm in excitement. Lord Fellon looked as though he might yawn in boredom. But the impassioned reader raised a hand in the air, denouncing power, encouraging the sharing of resources. He was quoting someone Charity was likely familiar with but Lucy had never heard before.

Lord Fellon snorted, and Lucy soon realized he was attempting not to laugh at the man.

Charity bristled beside her.

And Lucy wasn't certain what she should do.

"Of all the ridiculous…" Lord Fellon murmured. "The author writes freely of sharing though he probably has nothing. And he's likely never cared for tenants nor seen their misuse of funds. The resources are best kept in the hands of those who can control them well."

Lucy almost nodded in silent support of Lord Fellon as she was supposed to do. But she knew that a most respected sister believed the words spoken, and she Lucy had been the recipient of the goodwill of others. As a woman, did she not live her daily life, eat her food, and breathe her breath on the goodwill of others? What was so wrong with sharing?

"Perhaps I do not understand the full ramifications, but I hope to always share resources with those who are in need." She widened her eyes, wondering what Lord Fellon would think of her first attempt at a real conversation.

But he stiffened. "Will you disagree? When you know nothing of the financial dealings of tenants or leadership, when you've never sat in the House of Lords? From where does this suddenly elevated opinion come?"

Tears pricked the back of her eyes, but she kept her mouth from wobbling. "It was a question. For I do know the great difference a wise benefactor can make for a needy soul."

He stood. "Excuse me."

And he left the room.

The audience finished clapping for the final reader, and he still had not returned. The lords that had entered at his side were also gone.

"For what it's worth, your words were sure and educated and spoken with generosity. He is not used to opinions."

"Apparently not."

"And, sister, you are not the kind to be offering them. I don't think he will experience nary a whisper from you contrary to his thoughts, so he needn't become bothered. Perhaps you should speak to him?"

"But, Charity. I have thoughts. I do think and feel things. And they might be contrary."

"How often have you expressed them? Really, sister, I'm attempting to help you see that this new you is not the normal you."

"But what if I want it to be? What if I don't want to keep

myself so tightly laced all the time? What if I wish to let my hair down?" Who was speaking? Lucy or Mr. Sullivan? Did it matter? The words felt delicious to her ears. They freed the tightness of her chest as they exited. Then she stood. "In fact, I think I should like to say some more words to Lord Fellon before we go. If he's to speak to Morley, then he best understand me." She ignored the bit of protest that tried to exit Charity's lips and went in search of Lord Fellon.

It wasn't hard to track him down. His voice and others sounded out into the hallway.

"She was opinionated, she spoke bullocks as if she knew something about it, and when I corrected her, she refused to back down."

The laughter grew.

"As if she knows a single thing about any of it."

"I wouldn't abide her in my house if she wasn't so well respected by my parents, by everyone, the prince himself, though I cannot see why, not with opinions such as hers."

"At least she's pleasing to look at."

"Passably so. But if I wanted beauty above all else, I could have gone in any other direction."

"You'll be able to talk sense into her. She's never been anything but simpering and supportive until now."

"True, perhaps we shall avoid readings. And books. I should limit the use of the library, to keep such emboldening thoughts from her mind. The last thing I want is a woman thinking things." He snorted. "Or expressing them."

Glasses clinked together, and the men congratulated themselves on their conclusions. But Lucy's hands had begun to shake. She hugged herself, but her frame seemed unable to support much.

Gentle arms encircled her. "Sister."

"Charity. Let us go."

"Yes."

She led Lucy through the halls of curious eyes and out into the street.

"Where is the carriage?"

"They are preparing it, but it was taking too long, so I told them to meet us on the way."

"That's very untoward..."

"Does it really matter?"

Lucy opened her mouth and then closed it, shaking her head. "No. It doesn't."

"Lord Fellon talked to his friends about you?"

She nodded.

"And they laughed?"

Lucy nodded again.

"But we knew this would happen."

A surge of irritation rose up inside. "No, Charity, we didn't. We knew he wanted a duchess. We did not know he wanted a silent, unthinking duchess that he would humiliate in front of others." But her frustration soon died after the words left her lips. It was certainly not Charity's fault that Lucy had been so foolhardy as to express her true thoughts.

Charity held her closer until their footsteps were drowned by the coming carriage. "Our carriage."

"Yes, thank you."

They climbed inside, but as they approached the house, Lucy shook her head. "Can I visit the stables? Alone?"

"Of course. But it's evening. Will you be protected?"

"The duchess keeps a full staff. I trust them."

When the carriage stopped in front of the duchess's house, Charity exited and instructed the driver where to take Lucy.

She hugged herself, trying to stop the shaking, trying to

regain control. A duchess would not be such an emotional state. No one should know what was going on inside. She should be lovely. She should be gracious. She should sit just right. She should cross her ankles. She should pin her hair tight so that it never appears disheveled. At that, she felt herself break.

With hands in a frenzy, she reached for her pins. She tugged one out at a time. With each pin dropping to the floor, a new section of hair fell loose, and one by one, the pins came out until she ran her fingers along her scalp, reveling in the freedom of hair unrestrained.

She must look a sight.

And she decided not to care.

When the carriage stopped, she exited without a hand to help her down, and she ran through the doors straight to Firestone.

"Oh my love." She opened the door, closed it behind her, and fell on her horse, wetting her flank with her tears.

Firestone hugged her close, the feel of her mouth, her lips nibbling on Lucy's hair, more comforting than anything she could imagine.

She cried until there was not another drop or tear left.

And then when she lifted her head, she laughed. "Oh, what a mess I am, Firestone."

"A beautiful mess." His voice behind her, deep, loving, full of sympathy, filled her with hope.

She whirled around, not caring that her face was wet with tears, not caring that her hair likely stood out in all directions, just happy to see him. "Conor." Then she gasped and placed a hand over her mouth. "I'm sorry. Mr. Sullivan."

He opened the gate and stepped into the stall with her, taking her hand off her mouth. "Conor will do just fine."

She willingly followed the tug of his hands and rested her face against his chest. His arms encircled her, and her horse shuffled beside her, and she felt at once better.

With his chin on her head, his voice rumbled through her again. "What has happened?"

She shook her head.

But he stepped away and stared so deeply into her eyes that she could hold back nothing from him. And all of it came pouring out with new tears.

He handed her a handkerchief.

And she continued to tell him all, and the words grew and expanded so much that she shared her fears and her worries when they'd had nothing to eat, when people of all elevations and ranks would visit and they were forced to receive them with torn and faded clothing, how they'd had nothing to offer, but June had scrounged up biscuits. How she'd shaken in fear that one of her sisters would be taken from her in marriage and none of them with the funds to see one another again.

All her fears poured out without restraint until when she'd finally finished, she could think of nothing else in the world to fear.

And then a new fear arose.

With large eyes, she lifted her gaze to Mr. Sullivan. What must he think of her?

But the warm eyes that stared back into hers, the love that filled his face, the acceptance, more than that, the complete adoration reached her, filled her broken seams with something new, something delicious, something bold.

And that new boldness grew inside of her. She lifted her hands up his arms to his shoulders and stepped closer. "Can you believe I just cried a river into your shirt?"

"Good thing it's not a cravat day." He smiled and wrapped

his arms back around her, cradling her close while he looked down into her face.

"I hadn't noticed."

He wore work clothes. The clothes she'd seen him in more than any others.

"Lucy, I…" He paused, searching her face, his own a mass confusion.

"You don't have to say anything. I'm not asking anything. I just…I don't think I can do it anymore." The eyes she lifted to him were pleading. She knew they were. What did she want? She wanted to feel better. And she wanted him to know he was everything Lord Fellon wasn't. She wanted him to understand the great respect she had for him and that the son of a duke could be half the man of a stable hand.

And so she stood taller, meaning to embrace him or something, but her face grew closer to his, and his eyes darkened with a new kind of need, and she tugged at the back of his neck, that need traveling between them and filling her with urgency. Before she could think another thought, their lips were connected, and she was desperately, madly, joyfully pressing her mouth to his.

His arms pulled her closer, his whole body cradling her, filling her with a sense of safety, security. Everything was going to be wonderful. But that security was challenged by the tug of his mouth that felt anything but safe. The delicious danger that called to her from his mouth emboldened and tempted her like nothing she'd ever felt in her life. What did she need but him? There was no consequence they could not weather together. Her arms tightened, and his followed suit until she didn't know where she stopped and he began. Did it matter? They were one. They were together. Forever.

And then his kisses slowed and warmed her, the desperation turned to expression, and she knew, without words, that he was cherishing her with his mouth. Each pull of her lips, each pressure, each movement loved her, adored her, celebrated her. And she tried to respond with the same.

Until he slowed more and stopped.

And she had to breathe, slowly, completely, before she opened her eyes.

His gaze lit a path into her soul, and the love she saw in his eyes felt glorious. "Conor."

He smiled and dipped his forehead to touch hers. "I love hearing you say that."

They stood a moment longer, she just feeling, loving, gathering strength.

And then someone, a stable hand, called to another.

The reality of their situation sunk in.

And she gasped.

"Don't worry." He held up his hands.

But she worried. "What have we done!"

"Everything's going to be fine."

"Did anyone see that?"

"Why does that matter?" He was instantly affronted. She could see it all over his face. "Already ashamed of me?"

"No, of us. I could be ruined."

"To be seen with the likes of me."

"To be seen with anyone, like this. You obviously don't understand." She pushed him to the back of her stall and peered out into the main area of the barn. "But it looks like no one is here to see." The face she saw anew was stricken. "Conor?"

"What have I done?"

"You're just now realizing?"

"I had no right to treat you that way. None. I…I'm sorry."

"I can't regret it." She covered her face with her hands. "Never mind. I regret it."

"You do?" He approached. "How much?"

"I have to leave."

"Do you want me to walk you home?"

"No!" She turned, trying to soften her words. "No thank you. I think it best we not see each other right now."

"Ever?"

"I don't know." She waved him away. "I'm sorry. I don't know anything right now." She smiled and then chided herself, "But what kind of woman kisses the stable hand in her barn stall." She gasped again, avoiding his gaze. "I'm terribly sorry. Nothing is coming out right." She glanced at him again and then ran from her stall. "Please close the gate."

No one seemed to pay her any mind as she tore out of the stables and down the lane. Her feet carried her at a run for many minutes before she stopped to catch her breath.

And then she burst into tears anew.

"You have to get a hold of yourself, Lucy." Even her own stern voice did nothing to calm her heart.

If anyone were to see her in such a state, they'd think her ruined indeed. And she was. She'd done the unthinkable. She was unworthy to marry, certainly not worthy to be a duchess.

And glad she was of it. A giggle escaped. And then a new wave of shame. She had become what every single verse of warning she'd heard since a young girl had taught against. She should not be glad of such a thing.

Attempting every hour of every day to be the most proper of them all had created the least.

And…she gasped at the realization. She'd fallen in love with her servant.

Another cardinal sin.

Well did she remember all the stories of Gerald's almost fiancée who had created a way to be locked in a house with the footman she loved. For years, she'd clucked her tongue in disapproval at such a woman.

She was now that woman.

Her feet dragged on the road. She knew her shoes would be a sight.

And then Charity pulled up in the carriage. The door opened, and Lucy climbed in.

"Oh, sister. You have saved me from myself."

And Charity, bless her, did not ask a single question. They rode home, sitting close together, hand in hand.

When Lucy started packing her trunk, Charity packed hers. They faced the duchess together, explaining that because of a family situation, they needed to return home, and they were both on the road to Brighton by the next morning.

21

Lucy had been home at their beloved castle for two days before June entered her room. Her sister glowed with happiness and peace, and Lucy's heart ached that she would never have that same feeling. But at the same time, she exulted in the goodness of June's life. She deserved it like no one else Lucy knew.

"Lucy." June's gentle voice reminded Lucy of all the times she'd been more mother than sister.

"Come in, June." Lucy scooted over on her bed and patted a spot. "You look stunning."

"Oh, thank you. I don't recognize myself of course, but I do love to hear you say it."

"I think my heart might break with emotion when this new little one joins us. How will we stand the joy?"

"I'm not sure." June rubbed her belly. "I wish Mother were here."

The ache in her voice brought a similar feel to Lucy's heart. "I wish she were here too."

They sat a moment lost in thought. Lucy imagined June

had actual memories of their mother. And while Lucy did too, June's were the most clear.

Then June reached for Lucy's hand and leaned back against the headboard of her bed. "Tell me all about it."

Lucy let out all her breath slowly before she began. "I've really messed up."

June smiled. "I can't imagine it is so."

"It's true. Your most proper sister has done the most improper thing we can all think of."

June turned to her and just waited.

So Lucy told all, and nothing became more clear in the telling. She was filled with greater concern than before and came to an inner conclusion that she might in fact never marry.

But June just shook her head. "Now, sister, I don't see that you've done anything wrong at all."

Lucy's mouth dropped open long enough her tongue went dry. "How can you say that?"

"Well, I don't necessarily recommend hiding in barns to kiss the one we love, but he is a good man. You have leave to marry him if you like."

"What? He is our servant!"

"He was, but he no longer is. And his family comes from nobility, Lucy, he is more like us than we realize. But even if he were not, even if he were a servant only, and you loved him, we would support you."

Lucy couldn't really believe her ears.

"When I told you you could marry anyone, I meant it. My marriage, Gerald, Kate, we have all married well, and because of that, you are free." June's eyes sparkled with tears. "Which is just as I had hoped."

"But what will people say?"

"Say? Who cares what they say?"

"I am not like Charity."

"Too true. I know. This is the most unexpected of all dilemmas coming from you, but in the case of Mr. Sullivan, I believe that his station has risen to such a state that a marriage to you will only solidify his elevation and you two can live in a state of landed gentry status all your days if you so desire."

"And if he has no money?"

"I think he does, but even if he doesn't, the castle must be inhabited by someone, mustn't it? What better couple than one who both have ties to it?" June's smiling eyes and gentle words infused Lucy with hope.

"And Lord Fellon?"

"Well now, he doesn't sound like the right sort of man no matter what his title, does he?"

She sighed and shook her head. "He really doesn't. But he would protect us from social persecution. A duchess in our family would fix any possible problem we would ever face in that situation. Bringing in a stable hand would only further put us at risk."

"Not a single one of us shares that concern."

"But it just isn't done, June." Lucy's head dropped to her hands.

"It isn't *usually* done, no. But that doesn't mean it cannot be. You will just have to decide for yourself how badly you wish to marry him."

"I left him in London."

"He has returned."

"He has?" Her heart tripped over itself.

"Yes, but he's not called on us as yet. I've just seen him riding by, twice today. And that is why I thought to interrupt your isolation and talk to you."

Lucy smiled, a feather of hope awakening a new happiness in her. "I don't know if I dare hope."

"Happiness is a glorious feeling and not to be discounted. If you are offered such a promise of it, I say grab hold with both hands."

Lucy thought her quite right.

The next morning, Grace, June, Charity, and Lucy were sitting in the morning room when Morley stood in the doorway. "We have visitors."

The sisters stood, and the entire Sullivan family entered their front parlor.

Lucy wasn't sure what to think. She wanted to hide behind the sofa but was too curious and too disciplined, so she stayed put, forcing her hands to still. They entered. Conor was everything to her, just on sight. When she tried to read his face, he wouldn't look at her. What if he would not have her?

But he looked amazing, as handsome as ever. Even the tired, ragged face that stood before her was a wonderful sight to her lonely eyes. She inched closer to where he stood but not too close as to be obvious. The added steps made a difference.

"To what do we owe this visit?" June reached her hands out and invited them all to sit.

"I was speaking with his lordship and remembered our own attic might have clues to the history of our families and the castle. So I went up searching and came back with these." Mr. Sullivan lifted a wrapped packet of letters. "And we found something interesting."

Conor's jaw worked, and Lucy could tell he wasn't overly pleased with the findings.

Mrs. Sullivan clasped her hands together. "It really is the most romantic story."

"And the most tragic." His father nodded. He lifted the

letter on top. "I will leave these for you to read if you like. But this one spells it all out. Remember that line of O'Sullivans you have on your tapestry?"

"Yes." June's voice was breathless. She was always the most intrigued about their family history.

Because of Conor's reaction, Lucy already held the letter in great suspicion.

But he read it in its entirety, and at first, Lucy's heart melted with the great loveliness of the words.

"The O'Sullivan heir fell in love with and ran to Gretna with a local shop owner here in Brighton. And the letter we just read proves his willingness to do anything, be anything."

"Yes, read that one part again, the part about no matter who we offend, our love will carry us." Mrs. Sullivan clasped her hands together.

"Since you've already repeated the sentiment, we're good there." Mr. Sullivan then lifted another letter. "And here is the letter from the father of the O'Sullivan family. I will skip some of this for brevity's sake. Here. 'And so I must disown my own son, the heir to our estate, not because I do not love him, not because I don't wish for him to forever be in my family, but because he has broken his commitment to our family, to our estate, he has sullied our line with the commoner's blood. He has treated his royalty in a careless manner and has diluted the tie. And therefore, he cannot be allowed to continue as an heir producing part of the family. His mother is devastated, the woman's family is devastated. None of their children will be accepted. They shall have difficulty finding work. They will live in a half world, neither happy nor unhappy, and all for what? So they can say that they love one another? What a selfish manner indeed to treat their children and their children's children and forever after children. This ends the O'Sullivan line for all future generations. I'm expunging it from the tapestry, from the records, and asking all other relatives to do the same."

A great heaviness filled the air around them.

Lucy looked to Conor for some kind of reassurance, but he gave none. His face was a stone, rigid, harsh, unfeeling. She looked to June, but her troubled worrying of her lip between her teeth meant that Lucy would get no thoughtful response as yet.

Mr. Sullivan folded the paper. "And so there you have it. We lay claim to the name, the line. We don't hold the same squeamish principles, and it looks to us that someone in the family kept the heir close. And that is how the Sullivans came to be, and that is how we are working in the stables."

"That's excellent news." Morley leaned over to see the letters. "And these are magnificently well preserved."

"Yes, they've been in a box with a coat of arms and what looks like everything that might have passed from father to son, including this." He held up a signet ring. Lucy wanted to look at that ring. "It's the coat of arms. When the father died, the O'Sullivan estate went with him."

"Did they live in the castle?"

"Looks like no. There was a manor house near here."

"The old ruins?" Grace smiled.

"The very ones." Mr. Sullivan gathered the letters and stood. "We've had some wonderful good fortune in being recognized by the prince and in the new business we are working on, on the land we can afford to purchase. But I think we've all seen what can happen when one tries to step outside their lot." He didn't look at Lucy, but she wondered if he knew about Conor's and her rendezvous in the stables. Her mortification grew.

But Conor shook his head, slowly, almost invisibly, and Lucy let the relief comfort her but a tiny bit. The other parts of her would never be comforted.

So, if Mr. Sullivan wasn't speaking of her and Conor, what was he speaking of? She could only guess.

Charity shook her head. "Your situation is different from the original O'Sullivans. Your rank, your status in society has truly risen. The prince can create titles, he can garner social support. He can help you rise in station. If you are accepted by the prince, you are accepted. You are most certainly elevated. We were at a dinner with some of the most powerful dukes in the ton and the prince himself, a small dinner. And your son, Mr. Sullivan, was there. He is well respected in all circles and much sought after by the men and women of nobility." Charity put her hands on her hips. "He is not a stable hand any longer."

Mr. Sullivan looked like he was about to say something, but Conor shook his head. "Except all this experience in the much celebrated bon ton has taught me that being a stable hand is something to be proud of if it comes with kindness and integrity." He looked like he might say more, but he stood. "Perhaps it is time we left this good family to themselves, Father, Mother, sister."

They stood then and were walked to the door, Morley discussing all the while the letters and the interesting history. The last words before the door was shut were uttered by June, "Please come by again."

Lucy fell back into a chair, feeling empty.

"Well, I hope that helped clear your path." Charity came to sit beside her.

"Yes, I shall accept Lord Fellon's hand if he asks."

"What!" Charity shot to her feet. "How can you say that?"

"You heard the terrible misery the selfishness of one couple caused. I'm of the same mind as Mr. Sullivan. Conor is still suffering all these generations later because of their choice. He and I could marry if not for that first heir's choice. It is a harsh thing to do to many generations of people. I will do the responsible thing." She nodded her head and felt almost sure of it. And thankfully, she was strangely devoid of emotion. "And if Lord Fellon isn't overly impressed with my thoughts, my children and my children's children will be grateful." She should feel like a hero. She stood at Charity's side, kissed her cheek, and skipped up the stairs.

She got all the way to the top before the loneliness of her choice sunk in, but she knew it would come, so she was prepared. She cringed for a moment and reached out for strength from the castle wall. After a moment, it passed. She moved to her room, found paper and her inkwell with quill, and began a letter to the Duchess of Stratton, asking when the family would be travelling to Brighton.

fter five days, Lucy felt brave enough to go to the stables. Perhaps he wouldn't even be there.

But he was.

Conor saddled up her horse and even helped her up on it, all pretending he was nothing more than a servant to her. As she rode off, she could have screamed in frustration but told herself it was for the best. She was not going to ruin generations of her children's lives.

The ride was short, but that was all she could handle. Even riding felt lonely.

But when she lowered herself to the ground and handed the reins to Mr. Sullivan, she paused. "Conor."

He stiffened.

"What are we doing?"

His eyes shifted to her face for a brief moment, and then his gaze returned to the floor. "What is for the best."

"I thought so." She sighed and then walked out of the stables.

When she lifted her eyes, trying to be strong in the face of difficult decisions, Lord Fellon exited the castle and walked toward her. She gasped in complete surprise. "Good heavens." She clutched at her stomach. "I can do this."

As her shoulders lowered and her chin raised, she relied on years of training and pure grit and will to behave as she knew she ought so that by the time she reached Lord Fellon, she felt perfectly in control of herself.

Then without saying a word, he dropped down to one knee. "I was afraid I'd lost you. Miss Lucy, will you please be my wife?"

His hair was perfectly styled, his proposal perfectly proper. She was satisfied with the result of all her effort, and so she told him yes. "I will need a longer engagement. I don't see a reason to hurry."

"Shall I have the banns read?"

"Not yet." She fisted one hand, forcing herself to remain in control. "Let's have them read right before the wedding."

He stood up and lifted her hand to his lips. "Thank you. We shall make an excellent pair."

"Yes, I believe you're right." She smiled her most demure smile, which she had come to associate most with Lord Fellon.

They went inside and announced their good news to the family. Everyone drank to their health, and then Lord Fellon travelled back to London.

And only then after he'd gone, did Lucy allow herself a moment of panic. "What have I done?"

Grace came to stand beside her. "I think you've just made yourself a duchess." She kissed her cheek. "Congratulations, sister."

"Thank you." Lucy's hand went up to her face.

Hours later, alone in her room, she pulled a blanket over

her face and curled into a ball. Sleep didn't come for many hours.

In the morning, early, before the sun had fully shown itself, she didn't even don a riding habit but headed down as soon as she could to see Firestone. Hopefully, she would avoid all servants and most especially Mr. Sullivan.

But as soon as she walked in through the stable doors, she knew he was there. He'd left his touch everywhere. The placement of the tools, the organization of the saddles, even Firestone looked as though he'd brushed her down.

So when he stepped out from her stall, she wasn't even surprised.

They stood, staring at each other, not moving, until he rotated his shoulders, ground his teeth a couple times, and at last said, "You're engaged?"

Her lip quivered, and she wanted nothing more than to run into his arms. "Yes."

He nodded. "Will you be needing Firestone, miss?"

And nothing could have cut her off more than the donning of his typical servant persona. But she didn't fight it. She nodded. "Yes, please."

He gathered the saddle, blanket, and bridle in silence while she watched. She drank in the sight, knowing she might never experience their old pattern again.

He approached, reins in hand. The mounting block had returned.

But before she could step up and mount Firestone to ride her, he stopped and shook his head. "Do you love him?"

"What?" Lucy backed away. She did not want to be having this conversation.

"Do you love him?"

"Conor, I can't."

"Can't what? Can't tell me? Can't love him?"

"I can't be having this conversation with you. It's not right."

"I think I merit an explanation."

She nodded. "Fine. I don't love him."

"Then why are you marrying him?" She stared at him until he nodded. "Because he's a duke? Does he make you happy? Does he respect you? Do you even like him?"

With each question, she shrank lower into herself.

"Why are you doing this?"

"You didn't want me!" She nearly shouted the words; they came out of nowhere, surprising even herself.

"How can you say that?"

"After that letter? The whole fall of the O'Sullivan line. It was clear as day you wanted nothing more to do with me."

"Nor you me."

"You're right. We realized something important. Your father's right. This is for the best."

"And you're sure about that?"

Her mouth quivered, belying the words she must say. "I'm sure of that. I did the strong thing here."

He nodded. Opened his mouth, then closed it, then turned away.

"I can't do this." She let go of the reins and ran from him.

And he didn't try to stop her.

She ran out the doors and nearly knocked Charity down.

She held her hands out to steady her sister.

Charity frowned. "We need to talk."

Lucy sighed. "Fine."

Charity led her away from the stables. "Why are you doing this?"

"I just told him why. Because as was seen in the O'Sullivan letter, marrying beyond or beneath your station is a terrible idea."

"But he is no longer beneath your station. And our situation is different."

"I don't see that it is. Lord Fellon himself told me that Conor's social standing is as precarious as glass. He plans to sabotage him, because he's competition with his stables."

"That's ridiculous. He can't do as much as he thinks."

"But he can do something, and that's what made me realize. Lineage matters. It matters a lot. I'm doing this for us, the Standish sisters, for my children and grandchildren. If I raise a line of dukes, our place is solidified forever."

"But what about your happiness?"

"I'll be fine." Saying the words felt like a lie. She might not be fine.

"You will not. You will be miserable. And you will continue misery. Your children will be miserable. Your husband miserable. And all those dukes you talk about will be miserable."

Lucy shook her head. "You aren't really funny, you know."

"I'm not trying to be. A bit dramatic, yes, but, Lucy. You can live here. You can create the most successful stables in all of England. You have the blessing of the crown. You are in love. You don't need a dukedom."

Lucy wavered.

"Lucy, grab hold of what you want. Grab hold of your happiness. Now, while you can."

She wanted to say yes, but she paused and then her head fell. "I can't." Lucy walked away.

Charity said nothing more.

Two days passed before Lucy left her room.

No news, notes, or flowers had arrived from Lord Fellon.

And Lucy told herself she hadn't expected them to.

But she could not handle being cooped up inside. What would have normally been a comfort, a visit to the stables, was a risk, and so instead of riding her horse, she went for a walk.

The weather was brisk. The sky cloudy. Crows cawed a loud screeching call all around her and flew to the branches of the trees.

She walked down the lane next to the stables. She had no particular direction in mind and almost wished her walk would take a very long time.

The wind bit into her through her thin shawl, but she welcomed it to fight against the numbness that was threatening to take over.

Her walk continued almost blindly toward the small village outside the castle grounds, toward the tenants that helped farm the land, all the way until she reached the Sullivan house.

And when she saw it, she knew that's where she had been heading. But she didn't want to see Conor, not really. She certainly didn't wish to speak to him. She wanted to be close to something that was his. And his house seemed the perfect place.

"Margaret!" his mother called from inside the house.

Lucy realized just how likely she was to have to speak to someone, and she about scurried away, except that the door opened and Mrs. Sullivan smiled a large cherry-cheeked grin. "Why, Miss Lucy. Do come in." She stepped back and held the door wide open.

When Lucy approached, she gave her a quick squeeze.

"Begging your pardon, but you looked as though you could use a little cheering."

"Oh, thank you. I really could." Lucy stepped into the dimly lit home. As her eyes adjusted, she smiled at the quaint feel of the place. It reminded her very much of the home she and her sisters had lived in for so long. Delicious smells came from the kitchen which was just on the other side of an open door Lucy could see from the front door where she still stood.

"I apologize I've brought nothing to give you. I came upon the house quite by accident, I believe."

"Oh, that's nothing to us. No need to be bringing gifts every time you stop by." She waved her in. "Please come in and have a seat. I'll see if there's any more muffins or biscuits or something in the kitchen." She stepped through that door, and Lucy took the opportunity to get a better look around the place.

A set of narrow stairs led up in the corner. The walls were wood and glistened with evidence they'd been recently polished. The walls had two pictures on them that looked to be created by an amateur. But a talented one. A fire burned cheerily, and the whole of the place felt warm and cozy. She sat in the nearest chair and was pleased at how comfortable it was.

Above the mantle hung a coat of arms. Lucy recognized it from the ring and the other coat of arms she'd seen in her own rooms. The O'Sullivans.

Mrs. Sullivan entered again with a tray. "I've found some of our favorite jam as well."

"Oh, thank you. And you needn't go to the trouble."

But Mrs. Sullivan went to the trouble anyway, and she sat beside her as cozy as they'd ever been. "So, you're just out for a walk? All by yourself?"

"Yes. I couldn't sit still. I couldn't think of anything to do indoors at the castle, and I wasn't of a mood to go riding." She shrugged. "So, now I'm walking."

"I'm pleased as anything you found your way here. I'm sorry no one else is here to greet you. Margaret is not answering me. I wonder if she's gone out walking herself. And Mr. Sullivan is at the Royal Pavilion." She fanned herself. "I don't think I'll ever get used to saying that as long as I live."

"I can well understand. But I'm very proud of you all for your assistance to the crown."

"Well, thank you, my dear. They're working hard to make sure that your horses get the best treatment they ever have. I know my son Conor is over there himself most days seeing to them."

"He is too kind."

"I wish he was here to see you, but he went up to London again. He left not even an hour ago." She shook her head. "We miss him so when he's gone, but he said this was an opportunity he couldn't pass up."

"What's he doing?" She tried to sound as nonchalant as possible, but she wasn't certain she was fooling anyone.

"He's been offered a training position, some schooling. He'll learn business dealings and how to care for their new efforts. He said it would help him do well so that no matter what, he can keep his business." She shook her head. "I guess he just wants to be sure. These nobles are fickle folks apparently." She shrugged and talked as if Lucy wasn't one of them, which she appreciated.

"Well, that's very impressive of him. He seems to know more about horses than just about anyone I've seen in London, so that's also very impressive."

"He's always been preparing and talking about this. He's the reason we branched out of just running the stables in the first place, and now he's talking about being a landowner. I just don't even know what to think about that." She smiled, and Lucy felt the warmth fill her with a bit of happiness. "We're simple people here. We might know a lot about horses, but really, we're just all about family, and friends, and taking care of one another, and horses. That's the Sullivan way."

Lucy let her words settle deep inside. "That sounds so nice."

"It really is. There isn't much in the world worth worrying over except for those things. At least that's what I've always thought."

And Lucy knew that those were the only things she really cared about. Family. Friends. Taking care of one another. And horses. She laughed to herself. How simple.

Then she stood. "How long ago did you say he left?" The tiniest bit of hope gave her comfort.

"Within the hour, but he took a carriage, so he'll be slower than slow. He said these particular horses are not the best or fastest beasts."

Lucy laughed.

"And he did say one thing about you, miss."

"He did?" She held her breath.

"He said you were a smart woman, and if you were concerned about the difference in station, then there must be a real good reason. I think he's trying to even things out a bit, miss, begging your pardon for speaking so boldly. But he has a lot of trust in you." She stood. "I think you're most of the reason he's even ever thought bigger than his pa." She laughed. "I remember the first time he ever saw you. He came home and reported back on the new family that had finally come to live in the castle. Margaret asked if you all were pretty, and he said, I remember it clear as day, 'They're all pretty, Margaret, but there's one who is prettiest of all.'" Mrs. Sullivan smiled. "I know there's a lot standing in your way. And I remember well that story Mr. Sullivan shared. But I do know you can't find a more loyal man than my Conor."

Lucy knew she spoke the truth. There wasn't anyone more loyal than Conor. He would work hard, love her, and never speak ill of her until his dying day. What more could a woman want? "Thank you, Mrs. Sullivan. And thank you for this delicious jam."

"We'll send some up to the castle. It's my grandma's recipe."

"You are all that is goodness and kindness." She stepped to the door, breathless in her new realizations. "And now, I think I need my horse."

"Oh goodness me. That is quite a walk. Do you want to borrow our cart?"

"Could I? And leave it at the stables?"

"Certainly. It's just right around there, and the horse is tied to the fence. We haven't put him away yet."

"Thank you." She was about to leave but then stepped back in and hugged Mrs. Sullivan. She was the perfect kind of person to hug, just soft enough in all the right places. And squeezed her back like she really meant it.

"Now you be careful, my dear."

"Don't you worry about me. I've been riding my whole life."

"I know. That's the other thing he'd always say. 'That Miss Lucy makes riding look like flying. She was born to it.'"

Lucy smiled. "Thank you." Then she ran out the door. She

raced to the cart, hooked up the horse, and took off toward her stables.

Everything moved so much slower than she would have liked. But at last, the horse arrived at the stables.

"Someone, come get this horse."

Two of the hands rushed out. "Yes, miss."

"Please keep this here for when the Sullivans need it next."

"Yes, miss."

"And saddle my horse. Now. As quickly as possible for a long ride."

"Yes, miss."

She waited while they ran here and there, and after what felt like too great a length of time, Firestone was ready to go, stomping her feet and lifting her nose in the air.

"Hello, pretty lady. You ready to fly?"

The answering nicker made her laugh. "And now, it's time." She swung up onto Firestone without help and without a mounting block, laughing to herself about all the times she allowed Mr. Sullivan to help her up. Who could blame her, really?

Then with the most gentle nudge, Firestone was off.

Lucy took her on the most travelled road to London. But she rode for almost an hour before the hint of a carriage came into view. The closer she got, the more she wondered who was inside.

Would she have to stop every carriage on the way to London to discover which was this new borrowed carriage?

She approached and peered inside. Luckily, the window was open so she could make out two women inside. She smiled and kept riding.

Two carriages later, Lucy wondered if this was a fruitless

pursuit. And what would she even say if she stopped the man's carriage?

She was riding by pure force of will, second-guessing everything about her mad dash to London but not turning around until another carriage came into view, and this time, Conor's head peered out the window for a moment. Lucy laughed into the wind. He was there, right there. She'd made it in time.

She got closer and then made herself laugh with a new idea.

"Stand and deliver!" she shouted to the carriage.

The coachman turned his head slightly and laughed but kept riding.

"Stand and deliver!" she shouted again.

Conor poked his head out, stared at her for a time, and then called to the coachman, "You heard her."

The man shook his head and tugged back on the reins. "Whoa."

She rode up to the carriage door.

He opened it, his expression not readable.

"I'm going to need you to come with me, sir."

"Oh? And why's that?"

"You have something I want."

"Hm. This is nefarious business indeed."

"Yes."

"You only have the one horse."

"You'll have to ride with me."

He considered her a moment more and then sighed. "I suppose you've got me." He grabbed hold of the saddle and leapt up behind her onto her horse.

His coachman called, "Now what?"

"I need a moment, if you don't mind."

"Yes, sir."

"Bossing around coachmen now, are you?"

"I boss many people around. I see the appeal to having a servant." He laughed. "Did you enjoy all that bossing when I did your every bidding?"

"Are you not still?"

"Doing your bidding?" He looked down at himself on her horse and over at his coachman. "Yes, I suppose I am." Then he put his arms around her. "I hope you don't mind. I need something to hold onto up here."

"Hear that, Firestone? Conor is afraid he might fall off."

"I'm afraid of much more than that." His more serious, sincere tone tugged at her.

She turned to face him more. "Conor Sullivan, do not fall off this horse."

"There you are, lording it over me again."

"With good reason."

"So, my highway robber woman, what is it that you need from me?"

She let the question settle a moment. Then she reached a hand up to his face. "Your heart."

His eyes smiled back at her.

"Actually, I'm of a more giving nature than most robbers."

"Are you now?"

"Yes, I've come to give you mine." She swallowed, almost afraid of her own words. "If you'll take it."

His arms tightened around her, and he lifted her up into his lap, scooting forward more comfortably in the saddle. "Now those are words a man only gets to hear for the first time once in his life. Miss Lucy, you've had my heart from the moment I first saw you. I've done all I can to be worthy of you, and even now, I know you could marry much higher than

I, but if you want to give me your heart, I will treasure it as the precious thing that it is. I will never hurt it or take it for granted. It will be cared for and loved." He swallowed. "For all of my days."

"I know that about you, Conor. And as far as I'm concerned, there isn't anyone higher or more elevated than you. You've had my heart for a long time now."

He lifted her closer. "And you've had mine." His eyes held all the love Lucy thought she'd never have. He stared into her until she could doubt nothing coming from him, then he pressed his lips to hers. She responded with all the urgency she'd felt riding along the road to London, but soon, at his insistence, they slowed, and with gentle care, he kissed her from every angle, every press of his lips soft and asking, every move an offer. Until the world spun around her and she could only clutch him tighter.

"I love you, Lucy. Marry me." He grinned into her eyes, their lips still pressing in kisses in between the words.

She laughed. "Yes. I will! I will marry you."

Firestone tapped her feet.

"Easy, big girl."

The horse nickered.

"We've got to take care of our lady here, you and I." He patted the horse's flank. "And you. Can you be happy with such as I, truly?"

"Yes. Already, I'm happier than I have ever been. Thank you, Conor. Thank you for saving me from a life less than we both deserve."

His grin grew. "So now what?" He laughed.

"You still need to go to London?"

"No, I don't. I was really just running away from you."

"Then I say we go back home."

"In the carriage?"

"I'm much more comfortable right here."

"Excellent, but let's situate ourselves a little differently."

She laughed. And they found a way to sit cozily on Firestone with his arms around her and their bodies swaying to the gentle motion of the horse. The coachman was dismissed, and they rode home, going as slowly as they could.

23

The next day, Lucy wrote a letter to Lord Fellon, breaking off their engagement. Since no banns had been read, it was a much more simple affair than she'd predicted. He hadn't even talked to Lord Morley yet and might not be at all unhappy, besides a pang of disappointment that things were no longer decided for his future.

She and Conor walked together and made plans on how they would tell the family.

"We could just walk in and say, 'We're engaged.'" Conor laughed.

"And where is the fun in that?"

"Or we could ride in together on a horse, and they will all come to the conclusion on their own."

"I like this way of thinking. We could come in kissing on a horse, and they would know for sure."

"And we would enjoy that part even more, I think."

"It is decided. We shall be caught kissing while riding my horse."

"Of course, unless you explain yourself, I could be shot."

"Oh, true." She frowned. "Perhaps we're better off with the most boring method."

"Agreed. Shall we request a conversation with Lord Morley now?"

"Yes, I think that would be wise." She toyed with his curls for a moment, resting a hand at the side of his face. "Do you think this is going to be all right?"

"You and I married? I think it will be the most wonderful thing to happen to either of us." He paused, worry crossing his face. "Don't you?"

She ran a finger down his face and across his lips, looked deeply into his eyes, studied him for a few moments longer. "I love you, Conor Sullivan. I would be blessed indeed to be your wife. Yes. I think something wonderful is about to happen to us."

His grin grew. "I love you too, every bit of you." He reached over and tugged out a pin. "And I think I'll enjoy taking these out."

"Oh, it's going to be a handful having you around."

"But you love it, and you know you do."

"Having my hair down or having you around?" She raised one eyebrow to make him laugh, and it worked.

"Having your hair down."

"I do love it."

"And having me around." He took out another pin. And another. And the tight pressure on her head to keep her hair in place eased one pin at a time, until her thick hair fell in waves down onto her shoulders, and then as if responding to her very wish, he ran his fingers through it.

She leaned her head back into his hand. "This is amazing."

"Mm. I agree." He toyed and played and ran his fingers

over her head, over and over again, until she thought she might melt right into the ground.

Until they arrived at the castle and walked right into the courtyard. And then he stopped. "We must behave ourselves for this part."

"Yes, now that we are here, I should warn you, I do know he will be particular about who marries each of us sisters."

"As he should. And thank you for the warning." They walked in side by side.

A footman approached. "Miss?"

"Is the family here?"

"Yes, miss."

They made their way into the front of the house. The butler approached. "Good day, Miss Lucy, Mr. Sullivan."

"Good day to you. Is Lord Morley around?"

"He is in his office. Shall I tell him he has visitors?"

"Yes, if you could tell him that Mr. Sullivan is here to discuss a personal matter?"

"Very good, sir."

When they were left alone, Lucy turned to him again. "I love you. Tell him how happy we are."

"I will, and there are other things to recommend me."

She nodded. There certainly were. The number one thing being that he loved her. And that he understood her. And that they were immeasurably happy together.

The servant returned. "Lord Morley would like to see the both of you."

"Thank you." As she walked, hand in hand with Conor to tell Lord Morley that instead of marrying the duke's son, she'd chosen Mr. Sullivan, she couldn't even feel the old familiar worry. She loved Conor, and she had chosen to be happy.

The thick door stood closed in front of them. Conor squeezed her hand and turned to her. "Here we go." With a wink, he knocked.

"Come." Morley's voice sounded deeper, gruff almost.

They pushed open the door, and a whole room full of people jumped up in happiness, "Surprise!"

"What!" Lucy stepped into the arms of all the people she loved most in the world. Gerald and Amelia were even there. All her sisters including Kate and Logan. All smiling faces beaming love at her. The Sullivans stepped forward. As each person hugged them or clapped Conor on the back and called out congratulations, her love and confidence grew. When at last they moved out of the way and she and Conor took the two remaining open seats in front of Morley's desk, she could only laugh in happiness.

"Thank you, thank you so much." She turned in her seat to look into each face again.

Morley cleared his throat. "And now we will come to the business aspect of this meeting."

Conor looked around at all present. "With everyone present?"

"Oh yes, we're a close family here." Gerald chuckled to himself mostly, seeming overly pleased with the whole thing.

"I can't believe you all came. From London even."

"We love you, sister." Kate reached a hand forward to squeeze her shoulder.

"I love you all too."

Morley brought out some papers. "Now, first of all, we wish it known how pleased we are that we are adding the Sullivan Stables and the subsequent business to our family."

June stood behind Morley and rested a hand on his shoulder. "We certainly are. We could not be more pleased."

Morley leapt to his feet. "Goodness, June. My apologies. I didn't know you were still standing." He turned, looking for a chair, but there weren't any, so he scooted his over. "You sit, please. I cannot think with you standing there."

She sat with a wince. "Thank you. I was beginning to wish for a chair." She winced again and rubbed her belly.

"June?" Lucy watched her.

She doubled over. "Ooooh. That one hurt."

"That one?" Morley knelt at his wife's feet. "Have these pains been going for a long time?"

"Just since this morning." She smiled, but her lips trembled. "I think it's time to call the doctor." She leaned back, sweat lining her forehead.

The room erupted in chaos.

Gerald shouted to Morley and clutched Amelia's hand. "It's going to be just fine, friend."

Morley paused and gripped his best friend's shoulder. "It has to be." They stood together a moment, and then Morley turned to Conor. "To make a long story short, we want you to live in the castle. None of us will be living here. She has a large dowry, and with your income, you two might just surpass us all in wealth. Welcome to the family." He reached a hand out, shook Conor's quickly, and then lifted June into his arms. "And now, you, my brave woman, are going to bed." He kissed her brow with such tenderness it brought tears to Lucy's eyes.

As they left the room, Lucy called out, "I love you, June."

Her weak voice responded, "Love you too, love you all."

When Conor and Lucy were left alone in Morley's office, they sat in silence for a moment more. Then Conor laughed. "Will it always be this wonderful?"

Lucy reached for his hand and brought his rough and callused knuckles to her lips. "I hope so."

He surprised her and got back down on one knee in front of her. "Lucy, I will do everything in my power to love you until the day I die. I don't deserve you or any of this, but I'm willing to make it up to you every day of our lives."

She shook her head. "No, Conor, please. You are the best man I know. And the love we share is blessed indeed. I can't help but think it designed for our very happiness. Thank you for seeing it and for always being there, for the lengths you took to make something more of yourself when all along I should have just seen that everything I wanted and needed was right there in the stables."

Lucy leaned forward and took his face in her hands. "I love you, Conor." The kiss she pressed to his lips was tender, but soon, he stood, picking her up with him, and wiped all other thought from her mind. His repeated words were all she heard. "I love you too."

Read on for Chapter one of Pining for Lord Lockhart.

PINING FOR LORD LOCKHART
CHAPTER 1

Sometimes, secretly, Miss Charity Standish wished she could be like everyone else. Her maid Lily pinned extra jewels in her hair, gifts from the Duchess of York, who waited downstairs for her so they could attend the first big ball of this season. Typically Charity would have balked at such an extravagance and such an obvious attempt to shop her womanly wiles around the ton but as she turned her red locks this way and that, she couldn't resist the pin points of light as they reflected off the candles.

After the Duchess of Sussex sponsored Lucy and things went in a completely different direction for Charity's sister, and happily so, the Duchess of York determined to outdo her age old rival, the Duchess of Sussex, and marry Charity off to someone truly renowned.

Charity humored the effort because it gave her another season in London, access to anyone she would care to know, and the chance to build her reading salons and philanthropist activities. And come to find out, the Duchess of York was a secret Bluestocking. She had been for years, since the days it was on mode to do so.

She studied herself in the mirror, something she rarely took the time to do.

Lily sighed. "I wish you'd notice how stunning you are, miss." She laughed. "Everyone in the room is going to be watching just to have a look at you."

For the briefest moment, Charity let her maid's compliment have its way inside, boosting her vanity, but then she just laughed. "Perhaps I should wear a 'votes for women' sign as well then? Use the attention to garner some suffrage support?"

"Perhaps. That would certainly be something, wouldn't it?"

Charity studied her maid. "Do you think I should take all of this more seriously? Be about the business of getting married?"

Lily made a pretense of touching Charity's dress here and there before responding. "Now, it's not my place to say."

"When have I been a stickler for a person's place?"

"All the same, I remember my place. But here's what I think, plain and simple."

Charity smiled. Lily could rarely resist what she thinks.

"I think there's a reason you're so beautiful and it isn't just so that you can march around in your intellectual ways, telling all the men what they should think."

Charity's eyebrow rose ever higher on her brow.

"I told you it's not my place."

"And what is the reason for feminine beauty then? You too are beautiful. And you are not parading about the ton trying to catch a husband."

"Those opportunities aren't mine." She laughed. "As if,

the likes of me, parading about as you do." She shook her head. "I just think that you could keep doing all you do and be happily married while you do it." She curtseyed. "But that's all I'll say about that. You're ready and looking as beautiful as you ever have, if I do say so."

"Thank you, Lily. I couldn't do any of this without you. Nor would I try. If I do marry, it will be all because of your efforts, and that of her grace, of course."

The gown Charity wore sparkled to match her hair. The modiste had been instructed to outdo any other debutante that season.

And Charity hadn't been looking forward to that, but when she saw the gowns, she was admittedly pleased. They were beautiful in a manner she had not expected. They made her look strong and feminine at the same time. And she was infused with a new confidence.

She gathered her reticule and a fan to dangle at her wrist. She'd found the fan particularly useful if she wished to pretend not to see someone.

None of her sisters would be present at this ball, and none of her bluestocking friends. She was free to be and do whatever she wished if she liked, and a part of her wondered what it would be like to simply enjoy a ball. Must she always attend with a goal to spread important truths to the influential people in the room? Surely she'd done so enough; they all understand her standing on most things.

She tapped the fan into her hand. But there was that upcoming bill to consider. Logan, her sister Kate's husband, had sponsored it and where they assumed it would pass without problem, a few of the Tories were up in arms.

She stopped her thoughts. Perhaps she would just simply attend the ball, sponsored by one of the most influential women in London. If the bill came up, she would offer her opinion.

And Lord Lockhart might be there.

Her insides twisted up in excitable knots at that thought and she couldn't stop the rise of color to her cheeks as she descended.

Her grace stood at the base of the stairs as Charity descended, and the dear woman raised hands to her face. "I am enchanted. You, Charity, have far exceeded even my expectations." She turned to her husband who had just joined her. "Don't you think?"

He took a moment to glance her way, then nodded. "Yes, she will be a credit to your name. Well done, my dear."

Charity dipped her head. "Thank you both. I don't know how to appropriately thank such a kind gesture."

"Think nothing of it. Do good with what we've given you. That's the best manner in which to thank my wife." The duke's oft stern face showed off some of his laugh lines and Charity curtseyed to them both. "I shall do my best."

"That's a girl. And with a dress like that, and your natural beauty, I think the duke will be in high demand this evening, asking for introductions."

He grunted as they exited the townhome. "True. You might wish to thank me again at the end of the evening. That or conquer the hearts of every man there in one go." He chuckled to himself. "You know, her grace was quite the catch. I had to fend off many a young hopeful in order to win her affection."

The two smiled in a rare moment of tenderness toward each other.

The duke helped them both up into the carriage and as Charity adjusted her skirts, she felt herself lucky indeed.

Blessed. Thinking of Lily, she couldn't account for the different stations in people's lives, for their upbringing, for the incredible good fortune of some and the utter devastation of others. She only knew that where she had been given much, she must do the same in return.

They pulled in front of the Duke of Stratton's home. Thankfully, Lord Fellon held no ill feelings toward Lucy or the family for her sudden decision not to marry him. In fact, he may have been relieved. He was now courting a woman who made him laugh more than she'd seen a smile appear on his face, and the two seemed well suited indeed. If she were to guess, there might be an engagement announcement at the end of this ball.

She and the duchess entered on either arm of the duke, the doors opened wide to receive them. The house had been decorated with extra lighting. More candles than she'd seen anywhere lit the halls, the ceilings, the tables, everywhere she looked. And she could only be grateful at the extravagance. "Oh I do like to actually see a person while dancing."

The duchess followed her gaze. "Oh yes, they've rather lit the place, haven't they?"

"Indeed." Her husband's attention was elsewhere, to a group of men exiting toward what Charity could only guess was the card room.

"And what if Charity needs to scare away a scoundrel?" The duchess tapped his arm with her fan.

"Our Miss Charity has proven herself capable of handling any sort of man, but if something untoward is at risk to befalling our sponsor, summon me immediately. They will rue the day." The spark of protective power that lit his eye gratified Charity. She nodded. "Thank you, Your Grace."

What would it have felt like to come to these sorts of events with her own father?

She could only guess. So far, she'd been well cared for by her brother-in-law, Lord Morley, and dear friends. But for a moment, that protective glint in the Duke of York's eye filled her with loneliness by comparison. She'd not experienced much of that protection in her life.

She stood taller, but perhaps the Duke was correct. She wasn't afraid to speak her mind if needed. For this, she'd learned to hold her own.

All this talk of catching herself a husband had softened her. She looked around, needing an unwitting victim of her tongue.

But the music began, and Lord Lockhart bowed to them all.

"Why, Lord Lockhart." The duchess almost clapped with glee, and Charity wished she could perhaps mellow her response to the old friend.

"It is a pleasure to see Your Grace as always. I look forward to our next meeting."

She eyed her husband for a moment and then nodded. "I as well, that *musicale* was delightful." Her secretive smile made Charity laugh. She didn't know if the Duchess enjoyed their meetings more for the actual topics presented or for the intrigue of hiding her involvement.

"Quite right." He nodded. "And perhaps Charity will grace us with her singing at one in the not too distant future?" His daring expression told Charity he knew exactly what he was doing.

"Oh, there is no need to hurt the ears of all and sundry." She shook her head. "Come now. How are you, my lord?"

"I am well. Aunt Victoria is here, in the corner. And we are bound and determined to enjoy ourselves at this smash."

"Excellent. And how is your aunt?"

"She fares well. I heard this morning that all her gout and other ailments of the nerves have bettered just in time to attend. I'm unsure how long she will last, but at any rate, she seems pleased to have come."

Charity never knew if her ailments were to be trusted. They were convenient to say the least. "I'm happy you could come." She eyed him, waiting, hoping for the first set which was well on its way to beginning.

But he bowed. "Well, I am certain we shall cross paths again this evening." He turned to leave, and they were all aghast. Charity couldn't close her mouth at the surprise. "What?" She swallowed. Lord Lockhart always asked her for the first set. He had raced to find her, no matter who surrounded her, and asked for the first set.

But right now, he walked away from them, nervously adjusting his sleeves. What had gotten into that man?

"I don't know what to say."

'Nor I. Do you suppose he is intimidated by you?" The duchess looked her over. "He should be enchanted."

"Perhaps the lad is tongue tied. Happens to a man some-times, you know, when the lady is particularly beguiling." The duke nodded as though an expert on the topic of amorous dealings.

"I cannot account for it." Charity watched him leave the ballroom, growing more puzzled.

Then a group of the more handsome set approached.

"Oh, dear." The duchess fanned her face. "They can have nothing to be interested in here."

"Except perhaps she will be all the more beguiling to the others of their sex who might have an interest." The duke nodded to Lord Granvile who paused, greeted the duke and duchess, and then turned to Charity. "I did not know you would be in London for the season." He dipped his head. "Might I have this first set?"

"Certainly. It's always good to see you, Lord Granville." They didn't always agree, but who did Charity always agree with?

As she placed her hand on his arm and he led her out onto the floor, he grinned. "I already know this set will be the most enlightening and lively in conversation of any I have of the evening."

She laughed. But only nodded.

"Come now, what is to be our topic? Wellington's last battle? The state of the poor and the cost of food? Or is it to be women's suffrage? Land ownership?"

She shook her head. "Have we already addressed all those issues, you and I?"

"We certainly have and more besides. You are an uncanny conversationalist. I only ask you for a set when my mind is geering up to it."

"And so you are energized and ready for a duel of words, then?"

"I am if you are so inclined, but might I say first, that you are particularly stunning this evening. I could hardly resist the set if my mind were mush."

She dipped her head, strangely flattered instead of offended at the mention of her beauty.

"Thank you. Then perhaps we might discuss something that does not inspire debate?"

"Oh?" his eyebrow rose and the spark of interest in his

expression told Charity that flirting might be easier than she imagined.

"Yes, I'd be most interested to hear of your estate. Your family. You."

He seemed flustered for a moment, but just briefly. "Well, I'm honored to have garnered a particular personal interest in one so well read." He circled her in the set. "Then I shall tell you, all is well in the lake country. We do boast one of the prettier parts of England for my estate. Lakes, vales, flowers in bloom, plenty of rainfall." He paused. "And you? How are you and yours? The castle is well-nigh completed I've heard."

"It is, yes, thank you. We are all well. Mr. and Mrs. Sullivan are moved in to the castle and the stables have almost doubled in size." Charity shook her head. "Grace has opted to move to live with Lord and Lady Morley until her first season. And I move around between the two. Of course, now I am staying with the Duchess of York."

"Lovely people. He is also the man most apt to defend your causes on the floor."

"Is he?" She turned to find her benefactor but he had gone, the duchess deep in conversation with a group of her friends. "I did not know that."

"In truth, since talking to you, I've become much more inclined in the direction of universal suffrage. There is talk, you know, and of course the riots."

"And there you go, bringing up interesting topics. Shall we move on from the personal?"

"Are they not one and the same to you?"

She dipped her head in acquiescence. "I'm certain it seems as much." They moved down the middle of the line together. When they were facing each other again, she shook her head. "But tell me more of the lake country. I've never been."

She could hardly recognize herself. A perfect opportunity to cheer this lord on in his efforts in the House of Lords and she was bringing up the lake country? She couldn't account for it, except that she'd agreed to give this evening her best go at perhaps opening up personal connections with someone, more than one if possible. And, if she were being totally honest, she'd always wanted to see the lake district.

They talked of simple things, pleasant things, she learned all about his home. And by the end of the conversation, she felt almost as if she'd had a good coze. But she couldn't resist; as he was leading her off the floor, she pressed her hand into his arm for emphasis. "But I must tell you as well, I am most pleased with your efforts. If we can just get a large enough vote…"

He dipped his head back and laughed. "I didn't think you'd be able to resist. Yes, Miss Charity. You do not need to worry further. I have heard you and will do my best."

Only partly satisfied, she nodded. "Thank you, then."

"I take the role seriously and knowing that I represent you, gives me some motivation." He grinned and then straightened as though remembering himself. His bow was smart and he left her just as another lord approached.

Charity danced every set with a different man, and no sign of Lord Lockhart. Where had he gone? What was he up to? She eyed the door to cards, hoping he'd not succumbed to those trappings.

Finally, Lord Lockhart returned during supper. He was seated far from her, on the opposite end of the table, but their eyes met as he sat. He nodded once.

How mysterious. What on earth was going on with her friend?

She only half heard the conversation around her, aware more than ever of every laugh and feigned enjoyment from his end of the table. Until at last, when supper was over, she hoped he would come fetch her for a dance, but before she could say one word, he led another out onto the floor.

She froze in her steps. Would he go the whole of the ball without asking for a set?

He didn't look once in her direction and seemed as captivated as he ever was by the woman's conversation.

Charity shook her head and went in search of the duchess. Suddenly the ball in its entirety seemed tiresome. She hoped her steps were swift enough that even the bravest lords would not attempt to stop her in her path, but one moved to stand in front. Lord Wessex, in all his rakish glory, blocked her path.

"Excuse me." She tried to step out of his way.

"Oh, no, I'm pleased as anything you've crossed my path." He bowed. "Miss Charity. I've never seen you radiate so. I've been waiting for a chance to prove my dancing prowess. Would you please do me the honor?" His eyes widened, as though he didn't know every woman in the room pined for him. And then he tilted his head. "I do know you are much in demand and attempting to go elsewhere. I admit to hoping to dissuade that direction and distract you but for the time of this set?" His grin grew slowly and she knew nary a woman would resist such a look and as it turns out, she was sorely tempted as well. At least perhaps Lord Lockhart might see her dancing.

"And we can discuss any number of things. I'm at your disposal."

And that is what cinched the deal. She laughed. "You've discovered a way into my heart it would seem?"

When she placed a hand on his arm, his face, closer than she expected, grinned. "That is my very wish."

Her heart beat erratically before she calmed the ridiculousness. He was overwhelming in every way, but she must master her response to him.

The music to a waltz began, and while his grin grew, she tried to hide a groan inside. But he stood taller. "My luck is increasing by the moment." As he pulled her closer and his hand circled her waist, she knew she was in trouble indeed. Not for any minute did she think she might be caught in his snare, but he *was* certainly adept at winning a woman's affections and she was certainly not immune to them.

His eyes were the very shade of the Brighton seawater from the cliffs. His shoulders were broad and strong. His jawline was sharp, his cravat touching his chin in crisp folds of white.

When she looked back up into his eyes, they were grinning back at her in amusement.

"You are a beautiful woman, Miss Charity."

"Thank you."

"And I love just looking at you. I'll be open and frank. You're stunning. Everyone in the room is watching, women, men, everyone, you've captured us one and all. And I, am entranced." He led her expertly around on the floor.

She swallowed, unsure what to say or do in such a conversation.

"And I'm even more impressed as you refuse to simper and deny the hold you have on us."

She opened her mouth.

But he continued. "But here is my secret."

She waited.

He leaned closer. His breath tingling sensations down the soft skin on her neck. "I care less about capturing you for your beauty."

"Oh?" He'd certainly spent a good amount of words discussing something he now professed to care little about. "I appreciate it, naturally. But you." His smile curled larger. "I want to win your *mind*." His lips brushed her ear as he said them. Perhaps he'd done it on accident, perhaps on purpose, but she was struck by the wave of gooseflesh that jumped up along her skin.

"Oh?" She swallowed. Why could she think of nothing to say? Nothing at all?

"Certainly. You are my match in general appearance, but can I *impress* you?" He raised his chin. "I'm up for the challenge."

She had heard of this rake all over the ton. He swept through the women like a great tidal wave, leaving hearts broken in his wake. Just dancing a waltz with him would leave her open to discussion and speculation. The very last thing she needed was for him to enter in some kind of quest to win her mind. "I hardly think that likely." She wanted to bite the words back as they left her lips, but there they were.

But he was completely unaffected by her not so subtle rejection. "I know you have a notion as to what I'm capable of already, but I shall prove you wrong. I shall prove." He leaned closer again. "That I can be so much more."

They separated as she spun in a circle, moving around each other, her mind spinning with thoughts she could never say. How nice to entertain such a handsome man. He teased and tantalized her senses. His lips, so close. She'd wondered about them, thought about them. But she knew, every part of her knew, he was up to no good. That as soon as he'd conquered her, the unconquerable, he would move on. And so she said nothing. And she determined that evening to spend time deciding what to say in just such a situation when her mind shut off. She laughed.

"Have I pleased you?" He smiled.

"Not precisely."

"Oh? And just what are you feeling, Miss Charity?" His finger, ever so subtly ran a line down the bareness of her back.

"I'm feeling, like you speak the truth. You are a handsome man, Lord Wessex. But winning my mind will be a challenge indeed."

She'd meant to dissuade him but instead, his eyes glowed with recognition. "One I can hardly resist. You must know."

And then she realized her mistake. "No, that's not…"

"Say no more. I shall show you by and by." The music ended, and he bowed. "That, was a most informative dance. Thank you."

He led her to a frowning duchess, made his bows and then moved across the room, and out the door to the cards.

"Well!" The duchess fanned herself. "That was something to behold."

Charity clung to her arm for strength, to regroup. "What."

"Your waltz. I've never seen such a sizzling pair."

"Sizzling?" She shook her head. "He has said he will not desist. He wants to win."

"Did he now!" She grinned, obviously thrilled with something. "This season will be delectably entertaining and wildly successful if that's the case."

Charity didn't know how that would possibly be the case. But she did know she was in desperate need of a lemonade. And a chair. "Do you think…" She looked around her.

Lord Lockhart joined them. "Would you like a lemonade? You must be positively parched."

"I am. Oh thank you, yes."

The duchess smiled kind eyes at him. "You have arrived at the perfect moment."

"Have I?" He looked from one to the other in some form of confusion.

"Yes, where have you been?" Her eyes turned to him, seeking answers, but he shrugged. "I've been here, same as you. Perhaps not dancing with half the ton." His eyes held the same seeking of answers.

But she had none to give, and apparently neither did he.

"Can we get that lemonade? And then a chair? I might faint here and now."

"Well, none of that. No one has heard any of your treatises on the plight of the poor yet."

"No, they haven't."

"It has been an odd bit of a ball perhaps?"

"Certainly." She shook her head.

He seemed to be studying her more closely, but they made their way to the refreshment tables in silence.

The music began again. And once she'd downed the whole of her lemonade, he handed her another. But she now felt overheated. With her fan out, she looked about the room for a perhaps less crowded corner.

"Would you like to take a walk in the gardens?"

From anyone else, that would sound tempting in many ways, but from Lord Lockhart, it sounded like heaven. "Yes. Please. And perhaps there will be a bench, a nice cool secluded bench."

He raised an eyebrow at her. "Just what are you suggesting, Miss Charity?"

But he leaned his head back to laugh when she opened her mouth in shock. Then she swatted him and followed him through the ballroom, with more than a few looking on, out the back doors down the stone steps, and into the gardens. With light strung up above, and a quiet space, the cool of the night air caressing her skin, she breathed out in relief. "Thank you."

"Of course."

He said very little, and their feet walked in silence in the soft padding of earth beneath. They passed through an entrance of hedgerows that guarded a squared off garden space with a fountain and benches and roses to fill any romantic inclination.

She smiled. "This is lovely."

The bench did indeed feel cool on her skin, and Lord Lockhart was everything gentlemanly as usual. For once, his reticence to show emotion did not bother her at all. After the emotionally powerful Lord Wessex, Lord Lockhart was a soothing calm.

"I believe I've received some sort of odd proposal." He looked up to the sky, his face a mask.

To read the rest, Buy here

FOLLOW JEN

Jen's other published books

The Nobleman's Daughter
Two lovers in disguise

Scarlet
The Pimpernel retold

A Lady's Maid
Can she love again?

His Lady in Hiding
Hiding out at his maid.

Spun of Gold
Rumpelstilskin Retold

Dating the Duke
Time Travel: Regency man in NYC

Charmed by His Lordship
The antics of a fake friendship

Tabitha's Folly
Four over-protective Brothers

To read Damen's Secret
The Villain's Romance

Follow her Newsletter

Made in the USA
Las Vegas, NV
23 January 2023

66105194R00144